I0628391

OPHELIA

Book 1 - Lavender Cottage

by Mike Maykin

Published by Mike Maykin

OPHELIA

Book 1 - Lavender Cottage

by Mike Maykin

Published by Mike Maykin, Brisbane, Australia
mikemaykin@outlook.com

Other books by Mike Maykin
The Dark Earth series –
Book 1 'Nightfall'
Book 2 'The Rise of Sol'
Book 3 'Emissaries'
Book 4 'Almost Human' (coming soon)

Ophelia Series –
Book 2 'The Land of Frankincense'

'Deep Sahara'

Table of Contents

About the Author

CHAPTER 1

Ophelia tugged at the rusty farm gate as it bumped and scraped across the ground. She was small and it was big. Just another thing to fix, 'not a problem', she thought to herself. She knew what she was getting into, or so she thought.

The property was old and rundown, but the estate agent assured her there were no termites, or other structural issues, to be *too* concerned about. Good old honest John, the local estate agent, postmaster, delivery driver, and justice of the peace. The bakery couldn't make enough pies in a day for him to stick all his fingers into. He had waxed on about how solid everything was, tossing out clichés like, 'They don't build them like they used to.'

Sure, the cottage and out-buildings were old, and a bit broken, well actually a lot broken, but she could see past that. Her dream wasn't just the bleached stone walls and the cross-pane windows, as romantic as they were; no for her it was the lifestyle. Rolling up her sleeves and getting dirty hands. Planting, tending, and harvesting. And then she would set up a small workshop and make things for market. Maybe she would open a shop on the property, converting one of the barns to entice the many tourists that explored the region. Or she could have an online shop and sell around the country, around the world. Her imagination was rich, and the possibilities were endless.

She had done her due diligence, kind of. Having read 'A Year in Provence' and watched 'Under the Tuscan Sun' several times, and pretty much every other Netflix romantic chick-flick on the topic. Yep, her dreams were well honed and indefatigable. But what really caught her by the sleeve and wouldn't let go, like infant children are known to do, was how the property made her feel. And the one thing that turned 'maybe' into 'must' was the field of lavender that stretched from that old stubborn gate all the way down to the wooden fence surrounding the cottage. It was painted white, and the arch over the path was a tangle of climbing red roses. It looked like something out of a fairytale, like the cottage could have been made with gingerbread and candy, and in the garden lived fairies and gnomes.

Months before, during an evening of doom scrolling, she had seen its picture on a sales listing. The property had been an old couple's home; in fact, it had been in their family for generations. The advertisement read, 'Make your dreams come true'. Well, she had plenty of them, and they were all tugging in different directions.

There was the law firm where she worked as an associate; 'Catskill, Smyth & Peterson'. The possibility of making partner was real, or so she had been led to believe. Although of late, it seemed more like a glow on the distant horizon. They say work smarter not harder, but there is only so much rocket science in drafting submissions for the Family Court. The bulk of her workday involved reading about other people's lives, and how they got screwed over, or were messing up someone else's life. The Hollywood cases where the hero fights for the underdog, courageously tilting at windmills, were few and far between. What she was doing no longer seemed real or relevant. Now she wanted something that was tangible and organic.

Then there were the options to move to different cities, or even countries. There had been offers, and alluring snapshots of success, from her sisters and friends, invading and assaulting via social media. Why is it that *their* lives seemed more exciting. Was it just a 'grass is greener on the other side' type of thing. Did they look back at her with the same admiration or longing. Yes, she smiled in all the pictures she uploaded, but those smiles were just for the camera, a 'cheese' reflex. She wanted to wear that same smile when she was home alone, well actually home but not alone.

And that segues to another dream, or more to the point, circumstance that family and friends wanted to rectify, so maybe it was their dream; the *problem* of being single. She had everything going for her; didn't she? She was an attractive thirty-something lawyer with a wicked sense of humor and a kind heart. And it wasn't as if she hid herself away. Yep, she considered herself a catch, as she wriggled on the hook at all those business forums and corporate retreats. But would she settle down with another lawyer, probably not.

That man of her dreams, 'the man', he would be found among the lavender, not in a Southbank penthouse, driving the latest model Porsche. He was kind, not cunning and ruthless, as he dwelled somewhere in the right side of his brain. He was gentle, even when he was chopping wood, clearing brambles, and mending the rusty gate. Oh yes, back to the farm; she closed the gate and draped the chain over the hitch. It offered no security; it was just for appearances. Out here in the country, in fact hours into the country, on the high plateau of the Granite Belt, people still waved to their neighbors and left doors unlocked. So that chain was really just there to say, 'If I don't know you, then I would rather you didn't come in, if that's alright with you'. A clock was ticking, biological or some other, but the sound became so loud that she had to get up and move, and this is where she ended up. This is where she would plant her dreams.

She would get to know the neighbors and the shop keepers of Applethorpe, ten minutes down the road. She would live in a community and be a part of it. They would know her name, invite her over for lunch, and pitch-in when she needed help. That's what country people do, right? Then again, across the road was a commercial apple orchard, with trees shielded from the hail and birds by hectares and hectares of netting. They weren't really a granny and pop enterprise. And then on one side of her property was a large vineyard complete with a cellar door selling to the public, and on the other side were green pastures out to the horizon. Dairy cattle grazed and then plodded off to get milked. Even that was part of a foreign owned corporate conglomerate. Yet despite this, she knew the country folk were hiding somewhere, possibly in plain sight.

Ophelia's car bumped slowly down the long driveway. Her car wasn't really designed for this kind of terrain, being European and more at home in the city, and on the smooth freeways. But still, with some creative packing, and energetic pushing, she got a few weeks' worth of clothes and household items into it. The rest would arrive by van later. She actually hadn't kept much, but instead sold off most of her former life. She wanted to start with a blank canvas and paint a new picture.

Fortunately, it was dry. Winter had crept over the high country and that meant clear dry weather and those oh so still and frosty nights. It would probably get below freezing tonight, and she could already feel the chill each time a shadow blocked the sun.

Ugg boots, check, woolen beanie, check, and of course her puffy jacket. It was not haute couture, she'd left that behind in the city, but instead something practical that she had picked up in a local store. If it was good enough for the locals, then it was good enough for her. She parked the car in the shed next to the house. It was free standing, just, and she hoped it would still be up for at least a few more nights. She resisted the urge to push against the wall to correct the lean for fear it may collapse. She was sure a builder could sort it out, that is, when she had enough spare cash to pay for one. The budget would be tight for a while until she started to sell 'stuff'. She wasn't quite sure what the stuff would be, but she was optimistic she would discover or create it.

Key's jingled, although the estate agent had suggested they may not work. He just kind of handed them over as a formality, as part of the sales ritual. She clicked over the cobble stones, boarded by tuffs of tall grass, arrived at the front porch, and turned the doorhandle. It opened and she let herself in, finally she was in, finally she was home.

Honest John had said the power would be left on, so the first thing she did was try the light switch. No nothing, the cottage remained dim as the sun sank low in the sky. Perhaps another option, an old lamp had been left in the living room, along with a lot of antique furniture. She had made it part of the sales contract. It would have been hard to find items to match the olde world ambiance of the cottage, so she asked the former owners to leave whatever they could. She would sort through it later, restoring what she liked, and disposing of everything else.

The lamp worked; yay, power. That meant she'd have water, including a hot shower, and of course light. The next priority would be to start a fire in the old woodstove. It was the central feature of the kitchen; indeed, it was the hearth of the house, however, it was something she hadn't bothered to research. How do you start a fire without burning down the house? She was smart. She could figure this out, and if not, there was phone reception, so in a pinch she could Google it. But pride before reason, she would try to light it without help. It would make the achievement more rewarding and the fire so much more homely and so much more a personal triumph.

There were some old newspapers in the kitchen. They were obviously there for lighting the fire, so that would be stage one, scrunch up the paper and stuff it though the small firebox door. Now she had to find some kindling and firewood. Outside, perhaps she would try searching out through the back door. Strangely, this door was lock, but luckily one of the keys fitted and it opened easily, almost too easy as if it was ready to come off the hinges. Bingo, there was a small woodshed at the back of the yard, albeit relatively depleted. There was perhaps a week's worth of wood, as well as some bundles of kindling. Mindful of snakes and spiders, within a few trips she had brought what she needed into the kitchen.

It took her about half an hour to light the fire, and in the process, she filled the cottage with smoke. It was obviously a skill she needed to master. Well, on the positive side, she figured the smoke would drive away any wild animals and evil spirits. Hah, her own smoking ceremony. There were some dry stalks of lavender in the kitchen, so she tossed them on the fire, adding a pleasant aroma, and consolidating the negative into a positive.

So, thirty minutes lighting the fire and then thirty minutes of open doors and windows to remove the smoke. Not bad for a first attempt, but she would definitely need to improve before people started calling the fire brigade. Now with everything closed and the fire warming the house, and all before sunset, it was time to explore her nest. There wasn't much to see downstairs, just a large living room, separate kitchen with walk-in pantry, and then a side room that had been used as an office. She decided to also use it as an office, for her farm, or should she call it a study, where she would read, write, and research?

A single flight of stairs took her to the next level. There were three bedrooms, with the master having a Juliette balcony that looked out over the lavender that extended toward the back of the property. How perfect she thought. John had assured her the balcony was solid, but she wasn't so sure. It probably required a closer inspection before she stood on it. That would be something for tomorrow.

An old double bed with a matching wardrobe and nightstand remained in the main bedroom. She wasn't too keen on the state of the mattress but had brought enough sheets and blankets to cover it until a new mattress arrived. Very little remained in the other rooms, but that was fine. She would freshen them up with some paint, and then newly furnish them. Surely family and friends would be staying for weekends, or longer. She imagined running a guest house. Ooh the possibilities were endless.

The kettle was now boiling. Not an electric one but the large, dented metal one on the woodstove. It would be a cup of tea and instant noodles for dinner. So, there she sat alone at the old wooden kitchen table as the evening turned to night. Boxes and bags had been brought in from the car, and anything that remained to be done outside would have to wait till tomorrow. She braced a chair against the front door, and locked the back door, thus she felt secure for the night. There was a second fireplace upstairs in the master bedroom, but she wasn't going to attempt to light that and go through another smoking ceremony. Not tonight. Anyway, with all the clothes she was wearing, she should be warm enough, even if that meant sleeping with Ugg boots and a beanie.

So that was day one over with. The culmination of a dream, a possibility, a commitment, and then reality. This was how it was going to be, and she had to make it work. Just for comfort she lit a candle, and it flicked in the corner of the bedroom. She peeped out from under the blankets and watched the tiny yellow flame. For a while there was scuttling across the roof top, which was likely a possum, and there was a distant call of a bird. But other than that, it was perfectly quiet, no traffic, no neighbors, nothing. It felt unusual after living in a twenty-four-hour city for so long. Perhaps now she could gather her thoughts, both when awake and asleep. Maybe she would begin to write, perhaps poetry or a novel; to live the dream of pursuing her dreams. Happiness begetting happiness. She called her home Lavender Cottage.

CHAPTER 2

Dawn at Lavender Cottage, what a magical time. The only alarm being the birds and the coming day. As Ophelia stood in Ugg boots and blanket, she looked through the glass doors and out past the balcony to the scene beyond. The room was so cold! She couldn't remember if there was insulation in the ceiling or not. But still, even with the fires burning, it would take a few days to heat up the old stone walls and floor.

In the morning light she could see the frost. White, glistening and covering everything. She was keen to get outside and experience it, but not just yet. First, she would get the woodstove lit. If she was lucky there may be some hot coals left from last night. Maybe with just a bit of paper and kindling the fire could be coaxed back to life.

Yes, it worked. With a bit of huffing and puffing embers became sparks and then flames. This time it only took a few minutes and there was less smoke in the house. She had learned to use the flue controls and to get the air to draw through the firebox instead of billowing out the tiny door and into the house.

Fire done, kettle on, puffer jacket, she was ready to go outside into the brittle morning. She removed the chair barricade and opened the front door. If she thought it was cold inside the house, then outside was a whole other level of frigid. The air was absolutely still, even the smoke from her chimney rose perfectly straight until it got too cold to continue rising. The cobblestone path was slippery from ice. She had to concentrate to keep balance until her boots began to crunch across the frozen grass. She walked out to a concrete birdbath in the center of the overgrown lawn and poked at the layer of ice. It was probably going to take an hour or more of sunlight to thaw the morning out.

She had enough supplies on hand to make a rustic breakfast. Some scrambled eggs on toast, and a cup of coffee. Later, when the shops were open, she'd take a trip into town and get more stuff, and also try to organize a refrigerator. Of all the things that were left in the house, and some of them being quite valuable, a refrigerator was not amongst them. Apparently, a grandchild had fancied it as a beer fridge for his shed. Still, that fridge was pretty old and beat up, so maybe he was doing her a favor. She would now get something new and big. Yes, a big farm refrigerator to put all her produce into.

She took the back road into town. It was the roundabout route that allowed her to peep into people's yards, and to pass the shivering kids waiting for the school bus. 'Oh, what is this', she thought as she drew closer to a vehicle parked out front of someone's house. She slowed down to read the sign, 'For Sale $2,500'. It was a pickup truck, an old one, but it looked straight and free of rust. That was the kind of thing she was going to need for her farm. Provided it ran, the heater worked, and it was safe and reliable, then it might do the job. She'd still have her good car for longer trips and would use the pickup truck for dirty farm work. Maybe she could paint a sign of the side, 'Lavender Cottage' or something like that.

The situation with money must be discussed. Having worked long hours over the past ten years she'd saved enough to buy the property outright, but that didn't leave her with much in reserve. Her former employer had been pleased with her work and wanted to retain her services on a contract basis. Basically, they would throw some work her way and she could do it remotely from the farm. The post COVID world had ushered in so many remote interactions. Amongst them were remote court filings and hearings. So provided she had a good internet connection, and obviously her laptop, then she could supplement her income. And depending on how much work she took on; it could be quite a handsome supplement. Yet it was still that former life she was trying to escape, so the less time she devoted to legal work, the better.

She drove through Applethorpe and then onto the larger town of Stanthorpe, an extra ten minutes down the road. It was a bit like Europe up here on the fertile plateau, small towns were close together. In some ways it was like a micro-state surrounded by the vast distances and openness of Australia proper. The larger town was a busy regional center of stone single-story buildings build in the late 19th and early 20th century. Originally part of the overland route between Queensland and New South Wales, it was now a service center for the surrounding primary industries. These included apples, cherries and other orchard fruits, horticulture, wine, dairy, and tourism. Mediterranean lavender thrived in the mild summers and cool winters. Yes, it got freezing at night, but due to the subtropical latitude, when the sun came out on the clear winter days, it would warm the earth and the soul.

She drove past the only car yard on Main Street. There was a good range of pickup trucks and offroad vehicles, but the prices were way beyond what she was prepared to spend, even the second-hand ones. Perhaps she'd look through the classifieds tonight, see what the prices were like in the private market.

'A parking spot', she pulled in, grabbed her jacket, and headed off on foot. There were bakeries on each side of the road, which one should she choose? Would it be the one with more people because it could be better, or less people because the service may be quicker? It seemed that other bits of her body made the decision. She'd follow that rugged handsome looking guy that had just walked into the bakery nearest to her. He looked local, would likely have the appetite of a lumberjack, so probably the food was best at this bakery.

Oh my God did it smell good as she pushed through the door. The tree, I mean the lumberjack, sorry the gentleman, was already being served at the counter. All she could see was the back of his red-checked flannel jacket, and tufts of long, golden, wavey hair, flowing from the bottom of his knitted beanie. And oh my; those were rather well-fitting jeans that deserved a poke or a smack.

Someone was a lucky girl. Some ruddy country wench with rosy cheeks, a killer smile, and the skill to ride a dirt bike and drive a tractor. They would have healthy baby boys that would grow up to be tall and strong like their father but have their mother's beautiful blue eyes and kind temperament. Yeah, mom and dad were probably sweethearts in school, and got married in the local church. All the townsfolk were there and celebrated. And all this she could tell from seeing the back of his head.

"Madam, can I help you?" the girl behind the counter asked.

Ophelia had been so lost in her thoughts that she didn't realize that he, the man, yes that man again, had left. She ordered a hot meat pie, a cake, and coffee. It was her second breakfast of the morning, but oh boy did this cold weather make her hungry. She sat at a dining table and ate, watching the locals shuffle in and out in their woolens. They were doing a good business. A friendly and efficient bakery in the center of town seemed to be quite the goldmine. Maybe she could supply something to them and take advantage of their success.

On the wall beside her was a community notice board. People were advertising services, goods for sale, as well as various events. One particular notice caught her attention. It was an advertisement for trivia night at one of the local pubs. It was free and open to anyone this Friday evening. Perhaps she should go and have a look. It was a good way to meet the locals, make friends, and have fun. The alternative was to sit at home alone. Sure, she could find something productive to do, but more than likely she would end up just watching a movie or scrolling on TikTok. It was probably better that she engaged with the real world, as opposed to the digital one.

After breakfast she continued down the road until she came upon a shop selling homewares, including white goods. There it was, brand new in the showroom, her new refrigerator. She made it easy for the sales assistant by saying, "I'll take one of those," as she pointed to the unit. Then continued, "Do you have any in stock that I can get today?"

"Yes madam, we have some stock in the warehouse out the back. You can take it with you now if you like," he replied.

"Oh, that's good, but I'll need to get it delivered. Do you charge extra? I'm just at the old lavender farm on Eastman Road, about ten minutes out of Applethorpe."

"No, we don't charge anything for delivery. Will that be cash or card?"

She paid for the refrigerator, and a couple of other small kitchen items and then said, "So, what time will it be delivered so I can make sure I am home?"

The sales assistant flicked through a large book on the counter and then said, "You should see someone on Friday between two and four in the afternoon."

She said, "Oh, I'm sorry, there must be a misunderstanding, I wanted it delivered today."

"No, that can't happen, not today. I'd love to help you, but we can't do it until Friday."

She felt a bit frustrated. If she had known, then she may have looked for other options. But then again, maybe this was the only shop selling new refrigerators, and she'd have to get used to the pace and schedules of rural living.

She heard a voice behind her saying, "I could drop that off, I'm going right past there this morning."

She turned, and oh dear, it was *the man* from the bakery. Sure, it was a small town, but this was ridiculous. There he stood smiling, of course he was smiling, he was happy. He had a perfect life, with ruddy wife and all. 'Don't look at his fingers, not yet, too soon, not yet... OK now, quick glance'. He was not wearing a wedding ring; so that must mean 'she' was just his girlfriend, significant other, partner. An unbreakable bond that existed between them form the first time their eyes met.

His lips were moving, why were they moving, 'Oh he is talking to me', registered in her brain.

"Hello, is that OK? I mean only if you want. I'm picking up a couple of bar fridges right now and I'm going past your place, so it's no trouble," he said.

She turned back toward the sales assistant and gave a look of confusion and then asked, "Is that OK?"

Now the sales assistant was confused as to why she would even ask. He just shrugged and said, "Yeah, why not? If he's going past."

'The man', then said to the sales assistant, "Hey there brother, Trey Maccabee to pick up two bar fridges; they were specially ordered in last week."

Well, wasn't he just 'Mr. Cool and Casual'. It was bad enough that he had the looks, the physique, but now he had to be confident and casual, oh and did I mention helpful. Yeah, that's right, kind and helpful.

He turned back toward Ophelia and said, "Old

lavender farm, right?"

She nodded, like she was fifteen years old, and then smiled for a bit and then looked away.

He continued, "So, you'll be going back there now, because I'll be going past in about thirty minutes. Does that suit you?"

"Oh yes, I'm heading home now," she said. "I will go straight back home, and I will wait for you, with the refrigerator, you and the refrigerator, right." Did that come out right or was she blabbering? She started to walk away and then thought to say, "You will be able to manage, won't you?'

"Yeah, no problem. I've got a trailer and a trolley. No trouble at all. By the way, my name is Trey," and he put out his hand for her to shake. "I've got the eco lodge down the end of your road. You may have seen the sign for Lifecycle Retreat?" he said.

She took his hand. It was big and warm. So nice and warm on this cold morning, and in this cold shop. How could he have warm hands when hers were so cold. What would he think of her cold hands, surely, he would know that they didn't define her. You know, 'cold hands warm heart'. She was warm inside where it mattered, wasn't she?

"Hello Trey." That felt good. "I'm Ophelia, I've just bought the old lavender farm," she said.

"Oh yeah, the old Scott's place. I heard they were selling up and moving to the Gold Coast. Supposedly they have family down there, and of course its warmer."

"Yeah... OK...., well I'll see you soon," she said as he began to pull his hand away. Please just a second or two more, she thought. It will still appear normal, I promise.

She started to walk away toward the door, reluctantly. It is what normal people do. They act like they have things to do and places to be. She was busy, couldn't he see that. She had to get some groceries for the new fridge. It was very important work. Then as she opened the door, she said in an equally cool and casual manner, "OK, see you shortly, and thank you so much."

She couldn't find the supermarket, so she got back into her car and drove around. Finally, there it was, on the corner, so she pulled into the carpark and rushed inside. Stuff, stuff, stuff, where is the stuff. It was a small supermarket. The isles were narrow, and the groceries were not in a logical order. She only had a short time to get stuff for the fridge. The wheels on the trolley made a strange noise as she raced about. Some people looked and probably wondered why she was in such a rush. Ah yes, the fresh fruit and vegetables, the meat and dairy. Yes, a bit of this, some of that, just toss it in and keep going.

Damn, there was a line at the one and only checkout. It was painfully slow as the old shopkeeper talked to every customer. It was the same conversation, it always started with the weather, today, next week, this season, and then memories of seasons past. After that it would be 'what are your plans for today?' or something to that effect. Come on people, I have to get back home before Trey gets there.

When Ophelia got home the gate was shut. She must have beaten him. Again, she wrestled with the gate, but this time she would leave it open, inviting. But as she rounded the bend in the driveway, she saw a vehicle with a trailer parked beside the cobblestone path that led to the house. He had been true to his word; thirty minutes had meant exactly that. He was at the back of the trailer untying her refrigerator. It had been thoughtfully cushioned with packing so it wouldn't get scratched. How thoughtful, was it he who had suggested it, or was it the sales assistant? No, it was him. Because that's the type of person he is, strong but gentle.

By the time she had pulled up alongside his pickup, the refrigerator was off the trailer, and he waited with the trolley beneath it ready to follow her inside, or wherever she may take him. He greeted her just like any tradesman would. It seemed rather generic and impersonal; he could have at least used her name. He had remembered, hadn't he? His name was Trey. She remembered him, and his warm hands, and the eco lodge, everything. My God, it had been less than an hour, how could he forget so much so quickly.

"Hello," she said. "Once again, thank you so much. I really didn't want to have to wait till Friday. My life is already turned upside down with the move and all, so just a touch of comfort will be greatly appreciated," double entendre intended; 'Did you get that Mr. Trey'.

The frost had gone, and the path was safe, so she hurried to open the door as he followed with the trolley.

"I hope it fits," she said.

"We may have to turn it sideways. Some of these older houses have slightly smaller doorways. But it will be OK, there are rollers on the bottom of the fridge, so we should be able to manage," he said.

With a little effort, and fortunately no damage, they got the refrigerator into the kitchen, unpackaged, and plugged in. As the compressor hummed and the temperature dropped, Trey offered to help her bring in the groceries from the car. That eclectic mix of stuff she had gathered in a crazy rush. What would it say about her? Her whole life laid bare by the food she ate, and the budget brands she was forced to buy. Although there was nothing too personal, it was still all personal. Too late now, he was already at the car lifting heavy boxes of groceries as if they were filled with styrofoam and candy floss.

The awkward 'now that is all done' came and went when he commented on the woodstove, and how it was still alight from early this morning.

Perfect.

"The kettle is hot; can I make you a coffee?"

"Ah yes, that would be lovely, thank you," he said.

'Lovely', you say. Not just good or great, but lovely. Yes, warming, intimate and lovely. On my second day in my cozy cottage, on my lavender farm, you shall have a lovely coffee, and I shall make it for you.

"Finally, I can have it with milk and sugar instead of black and bitter," she said.

"Are yes, the joys of moving. I've done a bit of that myself," he replied.

They sat outside in the warm sun. A wrought iron garden set had been left in the garden. It needed a scrub and paint, but it was solid and serviceable. He didn't talk a lot, but he didn't hold back either. It's just that he wasn't the conversation starter. She would ask a question, and then he would answer, often in detail, and then fall silent.

Out of the blue he said, "You need some bees; I'll get you some if you want."

"Bees?" Ophelia said. "There are heaps of bees here. They are all over the flowers in the fields, and the early blooms of lavender. as well as the trees. There are bees everywhere."

"No, I mean bee hives. Your own bee hives so you can collect the honey. Lavender honey is in demand, there is supposed to be many health benefits. I've got some hives that I need to remove, so I may as well let you have them."

"Oh, that is very generous, but I don't know anything about bees, or looking after them. I wouldn't know what to do with them," she said.

"Don't worry about that," he said. "I can tend to them, or I know a bloke who can. Although, he'd want a cut of the honey, so personally I wouldn't use him. But hey, I can teach you. There is not much to it. I've got some spare suits, so you don't have to worry about getting stung. And of course, they will be beneficial for your lavender, in fact all of your plants. I can drop them off later in the week after dark."

"Why after dark?" she asked innocently.

"Because they return to the hive for the night, so that is the best time to move them."

"Oh, of course, yes, they are sleeping," she said with a nod, but she didn't actually know. Do bees sleep? It just sounded like the logical thing to say.

"Yes exactly, and would you believe they actually have similar sleeping patterns to humans. They sleep five to eight hours per night, have light and deep sleep cycles like us, and their body temperature drops when they sleep, also like us," he said with much enthusiasm.

As previously stated, Trey could go into detail on some quite esoteric topics, and then he would go quiet. Maybe he was shy.

"OK then, I'll give it a try. Are you sure it is no bother?" she asked.

"No not at all, in fact you will be doing me a favor. So, when should I came around," he asked.

"Anytime, I have no plans. If the light is on then I'm at home," she said.

"That's OK if you are not home. I can just drop them off. I'd leave them over there," he said as he pointed to a small rise on the far side of the property. "It would give the bees a direct flight path to everything they need," he said.

Oh, how sweet, he is even thinking of the bees. And with that he finished the coffee, excused himself and was gone. There were so many questions that she never got to asking, and information he did not share. Now that she had got some supplies, she was able to make a more substantial dinner for herself. She enjoyed cooking on the woodstove, it was just a shame that she was cooking for one. Maybe when Trey came back with the hives, she could entice him in for a meal. The cottage was starting to warm up, and after some reading in bed, sleep came easily.

CHAPTER 3

Ophelia worked from one room to the next cleaning everything. The kitchen was looking very homely with its subtle provincial theme. She had found some ready-made curtains in a country emporium. It was not the type of place, or floral curtains, you could find in the city anymore. She complemented them with copper pots and pans. It looked like she was ready to bake bread and roast a turkey; she'd have to Google how to do that.

There was a furniture store in town, so she splashed out and bought a couple of singe beds for the other two upstairs rooms. Fortunately, they came as assembly kits and fitted into her car, provided she left the hatch back ajar. The sales assistant assured her that the police wouldn't take any notice, especially if she just drove straight home, so she did. It was a bit of a chore lugging boxes of parts from her car to the upstairs bedrooms, and then having to follow instructions to assemble the beds. But eventually she finished them and was proud of the results.

All of these expenses were eating into the budget a bit faster than Ophelia had anticipated.

She had not realized how expensive paint and hardware were, but she figured that these were 'start-up' costs, as opposed to ongoing or operational costs. Still though, she may check in with her old boss and see if there was any work they wanted her to do.

Each evening before sunset she made sure she was home. You know, just in case Trey was there with her bees, and his hulking big..., generosity. It was now Thursday, and she had not seen him. It was just on sunset when she returned home. She was about to wrestle the gate in the still of the frigid evening and noticed the chain handing loose. The gate was still shut, but the chain was not how she had left it. If nothing else she was a creature of habit, and there was no way she would have left the chain dangling. 'Hmm, someone has been here' she thought, and then noticed fresh tire tracks that ran over the top of hers. They had been made by a four-wheel-drive, and only in the last two hours.

Trey must be here, and she smiled a bit and quickened her pulse, I mean pace. Yet as she approached the cottage, she could not see his vehicle, or any vehicle. 'Damn, he's not here', maybe she had missed him. She parked in the shed, to keep the frost off the car, and carried her supplies toward the front door. There was a loud crack; it made her jump. Then another one, and then a thump. Someone is here, and she quickly rushed for the door. She would get inside and put the chair against it. She made a mental note to get the lock fixed as soon as was practical.

The noises continued; sounding as if it were coming from the back of the house. She went over to the kitchen window, and from her crouching position slowly pushed the curtains apart and peeped up over the sill. There was a pick-up parked out back, and there was a man with an axe. He had his back to her, but it looked like Trey. She wasn't sure.

She pushed open the window and called out, "Hello, who is there?"

The chopping stopped and then there was silence. Perhaps he didn't hear her, so she called out again through the open window, while still hiding in the kitchen.

"Hello, can I help you?" she said.

"Hello, it's just me, Trey," he said. There was a pause and then he said, "I can't see you. I'm sorry if I scared you".

From her spy position she saw him lean the axe against the woodshed and gathering up splinters of wood for kindling. She felt rather silly and stood up to be seen through the window. He was wearing a t-shirt, and his face was a bit flushed. It was a strange site in the cold weather. He must have done a lot of work to get that hot. Again, she yelled through the window,

"What are you doing?" and then realized it was a rather silly question, his actions were completely self-evident.

As he worked, he called back, "The other day I saw you were just about out of firewood, so I thought I would drop some off when I brought the bees over. I hope that is alright. You'll go through twice as much as this over the winter. Also, you didn't appear to have any kindling left, so I was just splitting some down for you. Would you like me to bring some inside and stack it next to the woodstove?"

"Yes please, that would be very kind of you," she said as she rushed to open the back door. It was locked. Where was that key? That's right it was upstairs, and off she ran.

When she got back and finally opened the door, there he stood with a large bundle of freshly split kindling. She stepped to the side as he brushed past and put it into a box that was there for that very purpose.

Then he said, "I'll also bring in some firewood if you like. You have just about run out in the kitchen," he said as he pointed to the couple of pieces left in the wood box. And with that he did two more trips loaded up with logs perfectly sized for the woodstove.

"Do I owe you for this?" Ophelia asked as she cocked her head to the side.

"No, of course not," he said with a chuckle. "I get truckloads delivered to the lodge, so I've always got a huge pile. Most guests want a campfire, winter or summer. It's just part of the 'back to nature' experience we provide. So, I just skimmed a bit off the top. Really it was no problem at all," he said reassuringly.

"And what of the bee hives?" she asked politely.

"I dropped them off where we agreed, and they are all ready to go. There is nothing you will need to do, not for a month or so, and by then I'll have you trained and kitted-out. I mean only if you want to tend to them yourself," he said.

"Thank you so much, especially for the wood. I was wondering what I was going to do. And as for the bees, let me think about it. I'll see if I can muster the courage to do it myself." she said with a smile.

There was an awkward silence as they stood facing each other in the kitchen. Sometimes it only has to be a few seconds, like in live theatre when someone forgets or fumbles their lines. Something is supposed to happen, but nothing does. The actors just stand there in silence, while unseen their brains are swamped with electrons, chemicals, and dread. If she didn't say something fast then he was going to say, 'well time for me to go'. Not so fast buddy! The trusty kettle was hot on the stove, and she said, "Would you like a coffee; the kettle is hot?"

"Probably not a coffee at this hour or I'll be up all night, but a tea if you have some would be great," he said with a smile.

Yes tea, perfect. She had just bought some. It was in one of the bags of groceries on the kitchen table. She rummaged through and found it along with the biscuits she had bought exactly for this occasion. One day she would have home baked biscuits in a little barrel on the kitchen shelf, and little children would steal them when she wasn't looking. But for now, it would be store bought.

Time to get some answers while you dunk your biscuits, baby man.

Ophelia casually asked as she put away the groceries, "So, what's the story with the lodge, how did you end up running that?"

"Ah the lodge," he said as he leant back in his chair. "I bought into it just over two years ago and I run it with my partner," he said.

Partner! What business partner, life partner, romantic partner, he, she, who?

"Oh, that's nice that you don't have to carry it all by yourself," was Ophelia's tacit response.

"I do the day to day running and she does bookings and accounts. Yeah, it works out OK. We're slowly building up the business after it almost collapsed during COVID. That is why the previous owners sold it."

"Yes, COVID must have hurt many of the businesses that relied on tourists coming through the region," she mused.

"So, I am told, I wasn't here at that time. I was touring in the UK, and well that all got shut down. Actually, we were really lucky to get back home before the boarders got closed," he said.

"Touring, what do you mean by touring," she asked as she sat down across from him at the now cleared table.

"Touring with my band. That's how I know Francesca, she was in the band, and it was her idea to invest in the lodge," he said with a slightly confused look on his face.

"Oh, you're a musician, and you were touring. So, that must have meant that you were successful. Would I have heard about you or know any of your songs?" she asked with a small laugh.

"Yeah, probably. We got airplay on commercial radio in Australia a few years back, and we played support for a few big names," he said.

She continued, "And then after COVID you stopped playing and started a new career, or do you still do the music?"

"I needed a break. Sometimes you just run out of inspiration, and then things gained momentum in other directions. So no, I haven't had anything to do with the music industry for a few years now," he said reflectively.

"And then you and your partner, Francesca, took over the lodge," she said.

"Business partner," he corrected. "It's always been business, but she looks out for me," he said with neither a smile nor a frown.

What did that mean?

After another 5 minutes of small talk, he shuffled in his seat and then stood up and said, "We

I suppose I better make a move. I've got a few more things to do before I can knock-off for the day."

"Long hours at the lodge?" she asked.

"Yeah, something like that. Thank you for the tea and biscuits," he said as he opened the back door to leave.

Thinking fast on her feet she enquired, "What's the trivia night down the pub like, is it worth me checking out?"

"Oh yeah, that's usually a lot of fun. Many of the locals go there. Even if you turn up by yourself, they'll hook you up with a team. It's a good way to meet people when you're new in town. You should go," he said.

What did that mean? Does he want me to meet other people. What's the game being played here. He comes around and does all of these nice and helpful things, and then tries to hook me up with some 'local yocal'.

"See you later," he said with a wave as he headed into the rapidly gathering twilight and cold.

"Will you be there?" she called out with more desperation in her voice than she had planned.

"I don't know," then after a slight pause he said, "Maybe."

And with that he waved and drove away. She was both happy and apprehensive at the same time. That could have gone so much better, and it also could have gone so much worse. 'Now tidy-up and make dinner before cyber stalking him', she said to herself.

It was mid evening and for the first time she lit the fire in the bedroom. It slowly warmed the room and was comforting and romantic beyond compare. A new mattress had arrived, and her bed was freshly made with crisp sheets. No longer would she be wearing thick socks and a beanie to bed; it was becoming a normal and properly functioning home.

She sat up in bed and typed 'Trey Maccabee' into her phone. Scroll, scroll, scroll, not him, not him, not him. Ok, add musician, yes 'Trey Maccabee, singer songwriter for the band The Great Divide'. There were portraits and pictures of him performing. There were even pictures of him with other celebrities. He looked like a solid six-foot two country rockstar, complete with guitar and adoring fans. Wow, this guy was actually famous. No wonder he was surprised when she didn't know who he was.

She continued searching up his career, the songs, and the lodge. He had an extensive public profile, and it seemed he had never married or had children. Well at least that's what the publicity suggested. She began to play songs from the last album the band had released. The fire was the only light in the cottage, probably the only light for miles around. The heavy curtains were drawn to keep in the heat, and to keep the light to herself.

The bedroom was now like her inner self, freed from her mind to dance with the flickering flames.

She liked the music, and yes there were a couple of songs that she had heard on the radio. It had been written somewhere in the social media that a particular song had been used as a soundtrack in a movie. Did the songs say something about him, or had someone else really written them, and he was just the voice for someone else's feelings and imagination.

Quitting work had opened a new door in her life, as had buying the lavender farm and deciding to relocate to the country. And now it seemed that Trey had become another door. But this one was probably scarier and more perilous than the previous two. But then again, if she just forgot about him, then the apprehension would go away. It was a door that she didn't need to open. For now, she would just leave it ajar and see where fate took her.

CHAPTER 4

It was Friday and today was going to be spent in the garden. During the week Ophelia had bought a lawn mower and brush cutter. The sales assistant assured her they were easy to use and had sold her all of the associated safety equipment and accessories. She could do this; it was just going to be for tidying up around the cottage. There would need to be another solution for the surrounding paddocks. Perhaps she would need to get a contractor in to do that, although at the same time she didn't want to take on that extra expense.

She started the mower, it wasn't as noisy as she expected, and it wasn't too hard to use. The lawns around the house were not very extensive so she had them looking good within the hour. Then she started the brush cutter, clipped it to the harness that she wore like a professional, and then headed for the tuffs of tall grass. She started to swing it side to side and the clumps just melted away. Wow this was actually pretty good. Wherever, and whatever she looked at could be mowed down. So off she plodded around the house, the woodshed, the car shed, and then off down the trail towards the back fence, buzzing and swinging as she went.

After an hour she took a break. Surveying the work, she was pleased with her progress. The property was transforming from its rundown look and starting to appear lived in and loved. She walked over to the fence that bordered the dairy pasture. There was less to do, as the cows had pushed their heads between the strands of wire to reach the grass that grew on her side. As she was about to start a dirt-bike rolled up and stopped near her. It appeared like someone form the dairy was doing the rounds, checking the fences, and looking out for invasive weeds.

She could see him call out to her but couldn't hear him. So shut off the brush cutter and removed her ear protection. He smiled and said,

"Hello, I'm Reggie, I'm the dairy farm manager. You must be the new owner of the cottage. How are you going?" he said as he presented his hand over the top of the fence. He was a rather rugged and weather-worn man, probably in his sixties. He wore a stockman's hat rather than a motorcycle helmet, but then again, he didn't seem to be riding very fast.

As she took his cracked leathery hand she said, "Hello, I'm Ophelia. Yes, I've just moved in. As you can see, I'm trying to get the grass under control."

"Yes, you wanna do that before it starts to warm up again, otherwise it will be a fire hazard and the Council will start complaining," he said.

Fire? She hadn't thought about that. There

seemed to be lots that she needed to learn about property management. And they seemed to be rather important things.

She responded in her best faux country persona, "Yes, need to get it under control. Don't want any fires when it warms up."

Was that convincing? She'd just kick the tuff of grass near her to emphasis the point.

Then he pushed back his hat, scratched his head, and said, "Well..., I might be able to help you there, if you want,"

"Oh, how so?" she asked.

"There is a gate further back yonder," he said as he pointed down the fence line to the back of the property.

He continued, "I could open that up and let the cows in. They'd make short work of your paddock, bring the level down to what you see on this side of the fence."

She looked out into the dairy paddock. It looked like a manicured lawn, albeit dotted with cow poo.

"And what about the lavender, would they eat that?" she asked.

"Aw... just a bit," he said dismissively. "They'd mainly be interested in the grass and weeds. They would only nibble at the lavender and wouldn't seriously eat it unless there wasn't much else left. So, you should be right, and anyway, we'd have them out long before it gets to that. If they do start to chew on it, I can just string a line of electric wire around it to keep them off. Oh, and you'd have to be sure to keep your front gate closed or they'd get out on the road."

"And the cows, they aren't going to bother me. Like I'm not going to get charged and trampled or anything?" she asked.

"No, not at all. They're dairy cows; they are used to people and being handled. You leave them alone and they leave you alone," he said.

She didn't know if the dairy was getting a good deal out of this. From what she figured; they would be getting free use of her land. But on the other side of the deal, she would be getting her grass and weeds brought under control. At least if she didn't like the deal, she could always ask them to remove the cattle. It would be as simple as just walking them back through the gate.

Before saying yes, she asked, "You don't suppose I could get some milk? I'm not asking if I can milk the cows, but I was wondering if I could get some milk from the dairy. Not that I use much, but it would be nice to get something," she said innocently.

He laughed, more heartily than she would have expected. Had she said something stupid?

He responded, "Sure, how much do you want, because at the moment we're dumping about a quarter of our production, and our contract won't let us sell it locally," he said.

"That's ridiculous, what a waste!" she said.

"Yes, it is. It's partly seasonal, and partly to do with contracts and fluctuations in the price of bulk milk. At the moment you can have as much as you want, I just can't sell it to you, I can only give it to you, secretly."

"Oh well, in that case, maybe half a liter a day," she said.

Again, he laughed and then said, "Do you know how to make cheese, butter, or yogurt? And maybe even infuse it with lavender. And I see you've now got some bees; you could do lavender honey yogurt. I'm pretty sure you could sell that."

She had no idea how to make cheese, butter, or yogurt, but how hard could it be? Surely, she could just look it up. This could become a part of her cottage industry, especially if she was getting her milk for free.

"Ok," she said. "How much milk should I take?"

Again, he scratched his head and looked around the paddocks while he thought, and then he said, "How about we start you on forty liters?"

"A week?" she said.

He laughed and said, "A day."

This time she laughed and said, "No, no, no, you can drop off forty liters tomorrow, but honestly, I can't even store more than that. It would have to be forty a week until I work out how to even use that much milk."

"Alright, I'll leave it by your back door in the morning. And expect to wake up and find the cows in your paddock. I'll open the gate now and I'm sure they'll find their way in by morning," he said.

Then as he was walking back to the motorbike he turned and asked, "Do you eat eggs?"

"Yes, I love eggs", she replied with a smile.

"I'll see what I can do," he responded.

Then he started the motorbike and headed off to the back corner of her property, opened the gate, then rode off across the verdant green fields and out of sight.

Well, if the cows were coming in to do the gardening, then there was no point in doing anymore brush cutting. At least along this side of the property, for there was a lot of tall grass and brambles the other side that she knew the cows wouldn't be able to get too. Perhaps she should go inside and prepare for the milk.

She now kind of knew how Reggie felt about the milk glut. The cows needed milking every morning and night, whether he wanted to do it or not, and regardless of if he needed the milk. It was a white tide that could not be held back. And now she had joined the ranks. She didn't want to waste the milk, so it was time to research and develop new skills. Maybe this could be a new dream, or an appendage to her dream, Ophelia's lavender and cheese farm.

She spent the afternoon researching how to make various types of cheeses, butter, and yogurt. It all seemed much easier than she had imagined, especially if she kept things simple, like making cottage, feta, and mozzarella cheese, as opposed to hard cheeses which seemed more of an expert enterprise. But hey, maybe when she became confident, she could experiment with that also.

She went into town to get supplies, including a large multi-purpose electric mixer to make the job easier. Churning butter looked like hard work, but then again, how much butter did she really need, the answer was very little. However, like Trey and Reggie had gifted things to her, perhaps she could be the lady who gave her neighbors butter and cheese. She was liking this country life, and the productive potential of her cottage farm.

The previous owners had left some large pots in the kitchen, and industrial sized ones in the barn. She gathered up what she could find and brought them inside for scrubbing and sterilizing. Everything would be ready for tomorrow morning; clean pots, cheese cloth, giant ladles, and of course a plentiful supply of firewood to keep the woodstove burning.

It was early evening when she started to get ready to go down to trivia night at the pub. She had some 'good' clothes to wear that would also be warm. Because the property had a bore and a pump, the water pressure was good, and the hot showers were excellent. The notice said the competition started at 7:30pm, and she knew it would take her around 15 minutes to get there. She then figured that maybe she should arrive 15 minutes early so she could get put with a team, meaning she had to leave by 7pm.

One of the items she had fixed during the week were the blown lightbulbs. This included the front porch light. Now she could see as she clipped down the cobble stones to the garage, and she could leave the light on for when she returned later in the evening. She also had the front door lock repaired, so no longer did she need to rely on the chair for security. Thus, she locked the door and walked to the garage down the partially lit path.

She got into the car and noticed that the interior light was dim. 'Strange', she thought. She turned the ignition key only to hear a click. The engine didn't start. She tried it a few times, but it was the same. She checked the switches and found that she had left the lights on. How could she have done that; the damn thing is supposed to chime when you do something stupid like that. Maybe the chime had broken, was there a chime for the chime?

A flat battery, bugger! Fortunately, she had a small battery charger in the boot of the car. Also, there was power in the garage, so she could plug it in to charge overnight. Her father had shown her how to do that years ago. Sure, she could call for roadside assist, but it is usually an hour or two before they show up, and she couldn't even remember if her membership was up to date.

Damn, damn, she was looking forward to going out. Oh well nothing more for it, she'd just have to go inside and get changed, then come back out and put the car on charge. It looked like she would be in for an early night. Perhaps next week she would go. Maybe it was fate, and the gods were looking out for her, all for reasons not yet understood.

She'd thrown the clothes she'd worn that day in the wash, so all that were left, suitable for rummaging around out in the garage, were some super daggy clothes that she should have thrown away years ago. At least no one would see her hidden away in the dark on her little farm. So, after getting changed, and scrubbing one more pot that she had forgotten, she went back outside into the cold to put the car on charge. At least the battery wasn't fully flat, and she could see well enough to locate the charger. After popping the bonnet, she connected the cables to the terminals and then looked around for the power outlet. Yes, there it was, but oh no, it was too far away. The power cable didn't reach. Ok, maybe there was an extension cord in the shed? She knew she didn't have one in the house. That was something that should have been on her shopping list but had completely escaped her attention. She searched though the mess in the shed but could not find any power cable to make up the distance.

The next option would be to push the car forward, it only needed to be moved about 1 meter, but that would mean moving some of the junk in the shed. Yep, she could do this, so slowly she picked through it, making two piles. One pile for things she intended to keep, and the other for rubbish that needed to be thrown away. It was getting so cold that she had to stop regularly and put her hands in her pockets. She knew that if she went inside to warm up, then she probably wouldn't come back out until morning. Better to keep going, there wasn't much more to do before she could push the car closer and get it charging.

The silence was disturbed by the sound of a car, or truck, coming down her driveway. She looked out past her car and all she could see were spotlights, really bright spotlights that made her squint and forced her to put a hand up to shield her eyes. Who would be coming here at this hour, it must be at least 8pm. She didn't give a though about what she was wearing, the dirt she was covered in, or how the situation looked. Instead, she was like a rabbit in the headlights, just helplessly looking at the approaching vehicle with nowhere to run and hide.

Thankfully the car pulled to the side and then switched to the parking lights. It was a pickup truck, it was Trey. She stood there, puffed up like the Michelin Man with all of her layers of clothing. He walked over and said,

"Got problems, have we?"

Now, yes, now she became self-conscious. Here

he was dressed really nice, looking like a country gentleman, and here was her covered in dirt and dust, sorting through piles of rubbish. All she could do was laugh. The type of laugh you do when you are about to cry.

She said, "I got a flat battery so I went to put it on charge, but then I found the cord wouldn't reach. Ah..., so I need to push the car forward, but before I can do that, I have to clear out some of this junk."

"Oh," he said. "Sounds like a bit of an ordeal, let me help," he said.

"No, I can't let you do that. You'll get your clothes filthy. Don't worry, there's not much more to go before I can move the car," she said.

"Actually, I think I have a better idea. I've got a power extension lead in the back of my truck. I'll just grab that so we can get your car on charge. Then you can sort out this rubbish in the daylight tomorrow," he said as he headed back to his vehicle.

"That would be awesome," she said. "I'm freezing to death and totally sick of all this."

And like a superhero tradie he grabbed the cable, plugged in the charger, and solved her problem. He came to her 'little' rescue as to put it. She dusted herself off as they walked back to the house and went inside. In the bright light of the living room, he looked very smart, and she realized that she did not.

She said, "I'm so embarrassed. I'd put everything in the wash and then had to wear these," as she pulled at her clothes, "to sort through the rubbish in the shed."

He just laughed and said, "You're in the country now, these things happen. You wait till the rains come and you're covered head to toe in mud, or worse. We've all been there."

Then she asked, "What are you doing here at this hour?"

"When you didn't show up at the pub for trivia, I thought something may have gone wrong, so I just came back to check on you," he said while also looking a little bashful.

"Aww, that was so thoughtful. I hope it didn't spoil your night. Haven't you let down your team or something, won't you be needing to rush back?" she asked.

"No, not at all. I didn't join a team. I just thought I'd go there for a meal and to hang out. It's been a while since I've been to the pub. I'm usually too busy at the lodge. Anyway, the trivia will be just about finished by now, so there's no point in going back," he said.

"Oh, that's a shame. I would have liked to go, just to see what it's like," she said despondently.

"We can go back if you like, I'm happy to drive," he said with a burst of enthusiasm.

"Yes, let's do that. I only need about ten minutes to get ready again," she said as she rushed upstairs.

As she was getting ready, he called up the stairs, "Are you planning to do some cooking?" he enquired. "I see you have a lot of very large pots stacked up in the kitchen."

"Yes, the dairy next door is delivering a load of milk and I'm going to try and make some cheese, butter and yogurt. I don't know if it's going to work out, or what on Earth I'm going to do with it all. You couldn't use some at your lodge, could you?" she called back.

"Well, as it happens, I probably could," he said. "We've got a corporate group booked in for the weekend. I'm sure they would appreciate some local hand-made product. Will you be incorporating lavender, and in some way marketing yourself?" he asked.

"I'm going to try; I bought some labels that I'm going to print a logo onto. It is something simple and rustic that represents Lavender Cottage, that's what I'm calling myself, I mean the business," she said.

"I love it," he said enthusiastically. "I wish I could be here to help you, but I've got to go away for the next few days," he said.

Damn she thought, her hands would have to squeeze and pat the butter alone. And she would have to deal with Francesca all by herself. That hard-nosed businesswoman who 'looked out for him', extracting every last dollar of profit, and exploiting the poor honest hardworking peasants, like herself. Oh, it was so hard to be Cinderella.

CHAPTER 5

Trey's pickup truck was nice. It was almost new, really big, comfortable, and spotlessly clean.

She commented, "Wow, how do you manage to keep this so clean out here in the country, especially using it as a work truck?"

"Often, I have to drive guests about in it. We also have a minibus at the lodge, but it isn't suitable, or convenient, for all occasions, so this vehicle is the back-up. Hence it needs to be kept spotless. We do have another old bomb for the really dirty jobs, but I wouldn't dare take you out in that," he said with a cheeky smile.

'Take me out'. Was this a date? Had he been planning this, but then how could he have known I'd have a flat battery? Unless he caused it to be flat. No that's ridiculous, he didn't do that. He just had to take this car because he was wearing his good clothes. So that means he's just joking, teasing, and being cheeky. So that is a good sign, right?

Trey got out and wrestled with the gate, even though she had unbuckled her seatbelt to do it. That was nice of him. He took the backroad, and they passed the old pickup that was still for sale in someone's front yard.

Ophelia said, "What do you think of that truck, would that be a good buy for me? I really need something to use around the farm."

"Hmm, maybe. But at that price it could need a lot of work to get it roadworthy and reliable. It's been there for a while, so no one has thought it worth the money, but hey, you never know," he said, and then he went quiet for the rest of the journey, albeit short journey.

The pub was busier, and the people looked neater and more respectable, than Ophelia had expected. She had imagined it would be full of farmer laborer's and truckdrivers in their work clothes, half drunk and boisterous. But it wasn't like that at all. There were families eating three course meals, with children playing in a games room. People seemed to know each other, there was even a group of girls dancing to a band playing in the corner. Even the music was low enough so that you could have a conversation. It was the type of place she had hoped it would be. Whether it was like this all the time she could not tell. Maybe during the week, it was quiet, catering only to the hardcore drinkers, and maybe near closing time it got rowdy, and drunks spilled out onto the streets and the fights started. But she was here with Trey. He would look after her, because that's what he did, she had decided.

"Have you eaten?" he asked.

"No, I'm starving. Is the food good?" she said.

"Yes, it is good, but we had better hurry up and order, the kitchen will be closing soon," and they went up to the service counter and ordered. He got something rather small for himself. Maybe he had already eaten and was just getting something for her benefit, so she didn't feel uncomfortable being the only one of them eating. She went to the other extreme and ordered a mixed grill with the lot. Trey warned her that it would be a big meal.

She laughed and replied, "You haven't seen me eat, especially in this cold weather."

He smiled and said, "Cute."

Oh, be still my beating heart she thought as she floated to the top of the world.

During the evening, they sat, ate, talked, and had a few drinks. It was very pleasant. Trey seemed to know many people. They would acknowledge him as they walk past, and some would even sit for a few minutes and talk. He would always introduce her as Ophelia, the new owner of Lavender Cottage. She liked the sound of that, and also that everyone welcomed her to the area and wished her the best of luck. She felt like a debutant being presented to the world, a smaller, closer, and friendlier world than the one she had lived in before.

Trey disappeared for a while and then she saw him talking to the band during one of their breaks. He also seemed to know them. He was quite a different person in this social setting. Instead of the long pauses that she had experienced when she was alone with him, now he was full of conversation. Very much the social animal, and he probably had far less to drink than herself, so she couldn't put it down to liquid courage. It seemed that when he was around people, he came alive in a different way than when it was only the two of them.

While he was gone, she went up to the bar to get another drink, and saying to herself that it should be her last. She hoped she had the fortitude to stick to that, but hey, the night was going so well, so who knew. Why does too much of a good thing have to make you sick?

The singer of the band came over the microphone and said, "Listen up everyone, we've got a treat for you. Trey has agreed to do a couple of songs that I am sure you will remember. So please give a warm welcome for Trey Maccabee from The Great Divide."

He stepped out into the spotlight and there were loud applause and whistles. A bunch of women gathered on the dancefloor, not to dance, not yet, but to ogle, drool, and dream. She could barely see him for the forest of country girls, some even wearing cowboy boots and hats. 'Scoot ya'all, scoot out the way' she thought.

The band played back-up for Trey, and it sounded good. They pumped out some old familiar hits and the girls began to dance. Ophelia remained standing at the bar to get a better view. Yep, Trey still had it, both the sound and that connection with the crowd. How strange that he could transform into this confident and accomplished performer, seemingly at will. Perhaps it was all an act, for she knew this wasn't the real him. No light could burn this bright all the time.

A guy stood next to her at the bar and ordered a drink. While he waited, he began to talk to her. He seemed friendly enough. After he got his drink, he remained next to her, quite close actually. Perhaps that was acceptable given the music had been cranked up and the bar was crowded, but it was just at the very limit of her comfort zone. He asked a lot of questions and made a lot of bold statements. Was she supposed to be impressed? Fortunately, Trey was almost finished so she excused herself and returned to the table.

After a few minutes the man from the bar sat himself down next to her.

'Oh, dear this won't do', she thought to herself. Trey might think she's flirting with this guy or even planning to hook up with him. She didn't want to be rude to the stranger, but neither did she want to encourage him. Then again, Trey seemed to know everyone, maybe this was one of his friends and she was just being accepted into the gang.

After about five minutes Trey returned. He was very casual about finding her sitting with another man and said that he was going up to the bar to get another drink. And although her drink was still full, he asked if she would like another. That was thoughtful, but she declined. The other man asked Ophelia if Trey was her boyfriend. He didn't seem to know Trey, so she deduced that they were not friends.

She wasn't sure how to answer his question, so she tactfully said, "We came together."

It didn't seem that was a good enough, or clear enough, answer because the man responded, "OK, so he's not your boyfriend, and you don't have to necessarily leave with him, right?"

She laughed it off and said, "Oh, I definitely plan on leaving with him, but thank you for the offer, if that is what it was."

Then the guy said, "You know he's probably going to hook up with half of these girls later," as he pointed to the dance floor, "If not tonight then next weekend. It's what guys like him do. They spoil it for all the rest of us. The good guys who know how to treat a girl."

"Oh really," she said with a shocked expression and tone. What an awful thing to say. She looked across at the bar. Trey was standing there, and two women were talking to him. They were young, beautiful, cowgirls, and one of them had her hand on his bicep, rubbing and squeezing.

In an arrogant tactless way the man said, "Last chance," as he stood up.

Ophelia replied, "No, I'm fine thank you; I'll wait

here for Trey."

That bastard, she thought to herself. Why did he have to plant that seed of doubt in my head. She had been having such a good night, and a good week. She was really starting to like and believe in Trey. Surely, she was a better judge of character than that. Surely, she wasn't getting drawn in just to get used. People surely aren't that cruel? Well actually some of them are, and they usually look like Trey, and act like he was acting tonight. Damn, damn, damn, everything had been going so well. She decided there and then that she wasn't going to hook up with him later, no goodnight kiss either. Not until he proved himself worthy.

As she watched Trey, he seemed to excuse himself from the spiders and their webs gracefully, and within the expected timeframe. Maybe they had said 'call me', but he didn't seem to write down any numbers or accept any slips of paper. Was this what it was like to be a rock star, or the girlfriend of a rock star. Wow, it must take an enormous amount of trust and patience to be in one of those relationships. Maybe that was why you were always hearing about breakups and relationship turmoil surrounding musicians and actors.

He returned to the table with an air of normality and innocence, as if he had just been announcing bingo rather than singing and making the girls swoon. It all seemed very matter of fact.

"That was really good. I know some of those

songs," she said.

"Thank you. The band was easy to work with, which makes the job easier," he said with a smile.

"And the crowd loves you. I see you've still got groupies," Ophelia probed.

"Ah yeah, just the local girls after a few drinks. You have to walk the walk and be friendly to everyone, you know, give them just enough, and keep them wanting more," he said with a laugh.

What the hell was that supposed to mean? You're not supposed to be a musician anymore, so why are you still playing up to the female part of the crowd? Was this saying something about him or about her; was she being insecure, doubting herself and her judgement? That was not a good sign. She shouldn't be feeling like this so early into a relationship, or at any time during a relationship. He shouldn't be making her feel like this. He had responsibilities, like being mindful of his own behavior. To not act in ways that made the other person feel uncomfortable. Hang on. She wasn't in a relationship with him. He was just a neighbor who had helped her out. A friend who had offered to take her to the pub when her car had broken down. Oh god, no, no, no, she thought as dread washed over her. Was this what it was like to fall for someone?

No, it was too early. She had so much work to do on the farm, and dreams to chase. She had milk being delivered tomorrow morning, and labels to print that read 'Lavender Cottage'. Why do these things hit you when you are not looking. Fortunately, he was going away for the next few days; she could get her boat back on an even keel before he returned.

The drive home was cordial, and conversation centered around his trip to the Gold Coast. Based on his detailed description, it was purely business and something that he wasn't terribly looking forward to.

As they drove down her driveway she asked, "So have you written any more songs since you stopped doing music full time?"

"No," he said. "I haven't written anything for a while. Just haven't been inspired. Of course, then when you are busy with work, even if you have the slightest spark of inspiration, there is no time to build on it. Time is like tinder for the fire. If you have lots of time, like quiet time when your mind can wander, that is when you start to do creative things. Look at your own situation. You have removed yourself from distractions and given yourself time. I know that you have been really busy at the cottage, but what I mean is that you removed yourself from your past life and all of its distractions. Now look what you have, and will, achieve. I think you are amazing."

And then the truck stopped out front of her cottage, right when he said the word 'amazing', and it was time for her to get out and go inside. He got out and walked her to the door, but he kept his distance as if he was dropping off a guest at the lodge. She casually asked if he wanted to come inside. He thanked her but said he really needed to get home because he had an early start in the morning. What!? This girl just asked you to come inside. What the hell!? Was he playing with her, playing hard to get. Him, doing that to her?

Ophelia maintained her composure, standing in the doorway as he walked back to the truck. He stopped and turned, wishing her luck with the cheese and everything else tomorrow morning.

Then he said, thankfully, "I'll see you in a few days."

She would look forward to that and smiled as she closed the door. She put some wood on both fires and then slipped into bed. Everything was happening so fast, and ironically since she had 'supposedly' slowed down the pace of her life. So, he would see her in a few days. That meant he wanted to see her again, he must like her, and have respect for her; good.

CHAPTER 6

The thermometer outside the back door read minus five degrees centigrade. It was light but the sun had not yet risen. The dawn air was still, and everything was covered in white frost. Next to the step were ten one-gallon plastic jugs of milk. They looked like the type delivered to a commercial kitchen or a factory. There were also two cartons of eggs, therefore two-dozen hens' eggs. 'Oh, my goodness', Ophelia thought. She would be having eggs for breakfast every day, or maybe she could cook with them. Perhaps make baked cheesecake, sprinkled with lavender petals, this would mean she would have to add cream cheese to her production line.

She hefted everything inside and prepared for work. The first thing being to stoke the fire and put on an apron. She had never worn an apron before, and probably didn't need it, but it felt good to wear as it signified serious intent. She put several big pots onto the woodstove. It had a wide cast-iron surface that could accommodated several pots at once. She poured in some of the milk and fitted thermometers so that different pots would be brought to different temperatures depending on what was going to be made.

The milk had been pasteurized but not homogenized, hence there was a thick layer of cream on the top. Thus, with the remainder of the milk, she skimmed the cream off the top to be used for making butter. After collecting as much as she thought necessary, she began putting batches through the electric blender on its way to solidifying into butter.

After a full morning of work she had achieved the following: eight 250g blocks of butter, neatly wrapped in waxy paper, and sealed with a Lavender Cottage sticky label; ten 250g tubs of cottage cheese, three of 250g tubs of cream cheese, five 200g blocks of feta, and five 200g balls of mozzarella. She had also set aside, near the woodstove for warmth, two clay crockpots of yogurt cultured milk for setting. These would take up to twelve hours before they were ready.

Ophelia stood back and surveyed the kitchen. She was extremely pleased with her effort and the results. This cooking gig wasn't so bad, especially if you are doing it for your own satisfaction. Maybe tomorrow she would have a crack at making some baked cheesecakes. It would be her first time using the woodstove oven; how hard could it be?

She packed some of the cheeses and butter into a carton, changed into some respectable clothes, loaded the car, and then headed out. It was a fifteen-minute drive to the lodge. About five minutes was on the paved road, but the remaining ten minutes was on a single lane dirt track. It wound through scrubland and then climbed higher and higher onto an open granite-boulder plateau. Finally, she could see the buildings. There was the main lodge, come convention center, and then a collection of cabins. They were on the edge of the plateau looking out across a broad valley. It faced West and no doubt the sunsets must have been stunning. And in the late spring, when the thunderstorm rolled in from the Southwest, it would have provided a stadium-like view.

She pulled up to the entrance of a building signposted as reception. With her carton of produce she walked up the steps and went inside. It was very open and tranquil with a wall of glass that looked out over the valley and distant mountains. A water feature bubbled near the door and meditative music played through a hidden speaker system. Further inside the main lounge area people sat talking. They appeared to be guests that had recently returned from a hike, warming themselves by a large log fire in the center of the room.

There was a lady seated behind the reception counter talking on the telephone. It sounded like she was taking a booking for a month or two in the future. As the person on the other end of the phone suggested dates, she would say that they were already booked, or that there wouldn't be enough cabins. Eventually they settled on a date, other information was exchanged, and the deal was sealed.

Ophelia was looking at a picture on the wall, a beautiful, framed photograph from a local photographer, being sold for a handsome sum of money.

She heard the lady say, "Hello, can I help you?"

"Hello, I've got some cheese and butter for the lodge. Trey suggested you may want some," she said in her friendliest peasant voice.

"Oh?" the lady said, changing from the polite receptionist, keen to please and book clients, to an officious gatekeeper.

"He didn't mention anything to me, and he's not here at the moment so I can't ask him about it," she said.

Ophelia said, "Well, it was all very informal and last minute so maybe he forgot. Could you maybe call him?" she suggested.

"No, I can't call him," she said without explanation, then continued, "And where are you from?"

"I'm from just down the road at Lavender Cottage. These are all home made," she said as she took out some butter and cheese and put then on the counter.

The lady looked at them and then said, "I'm not aware we have an account with you, have we bought from you before?"

"No, no, not at all. I have just moved in and ...,"

The lady spoke over her, "I'm sorry but I cannot buy these from you unless you have an account, and anyway, we only purchase from producers that have been certified as organic. You will need to go through our normal process before we can take you on as a supplier."

"But I'm not here to sell you anything, I'm giving them to you, I'm here to help out. Trey said that you could use these and so I made them fresh this morning, and I have delivered them here as early as I could," she said with a frustrated plea.

"I see," said the lady with neither a smile nor a thank you.

Then she said, "Then you can leave them just over there, *please*," and she pointed to an area that appeared to be for deliveries, next to a door that said, 'staff only'. It was probably the entrance to the kitchen.

Ophelia said, "They will need to be refrigerated or they will spoil. Also, they don't contain any preservatives, so they only have a limited shelf-life."

"Thank you," said the lady in a dismissive tone as she picked up the phone to make another call.

Ophelia put down the box, and as she turned to leave asked, "May I have your name, just so I know who received the goods?"

"Francesca, I'm the owner," she said as she began to dial the phone.

Ophelia walked back to her car feeling deflated and a bit angry. She had been so enthusiastic, and then just one person with a frigid demeanor, and delusions of superiority, spoiled her day. In her mind she had imagined walking in with her produce and getting complemented by the chef. The staff sampling the goods and saying that it was the best they had ever tasted. And then they saying they wanted as much as she could make. She saw herself building a thriving business, with Lavender Cottage food and fragrances gracing the finest tables around the world.

Dreams motivated people like her to achieve, and deflated dreams could be paralyzing. She couldn't let this get her down. It must be just a big misunderstanding. Trey will sort it out when he gets back, she was sure of that. What had he said about Francesca, that she 'looked out for him'. Maybe that is what he meant, and what she was doing. Still though, it was very rude, and she deserved to be treated better than that. Everyone deserves to be treated better than that.

As Ophelia drove back down the winding track to the main road, the phone rang. It was the boss form her former law firm. This was rather a surprise given it was a Saturday afternoon. They had always been sticklers for down-time on the weekends.

She took the call, "Hello, this is Ophelia."

"Hello, it's Dee here, how are you?"

"Hi, I'm well thank you, but it's taking a bit to get used to the cold up here," Ophelia said.

"Yes, I bet it is. How is your cottage coming along, is it warm?" Dee enquired.

"Oh yes, its lovely and warm, but I have to keep at least one fire constantly burning," she said.

"And how are you settling in, have you got everything cleaned up and organized? I remember you saying that the previous owners were going to leave a lot of stuff there for you to sort through," Dee said.

"Yes, I've got the house sorted, but there is still a lot of junk out in the sheds and barn. There are some antiques and treasures amongst it, but most of it is just rubbish and will have to go down the tip," she said.

"And when will you get the delivery of your remaining stuff?" Dee enquired.

"That will probably be on Monday, although there's not too much. It's mainly clothes and small pieces of furniture that I couldn't fit in the car," she replied.

"Ophelia, I'll tell you why I'm calling. Now you can say no, and no one will think the worse of you for it, but we need a big favor. I'm wondering if you could put someone up for a week. It's to do with the Bianchi case. I can't really tell you too much, and I know that this is a rather unusual request, but we need a witness to disappear for the week," Dee said.

"Oh…, that sounds rather serious. Who is it?" she asked.

"Her name is Stella. We just need to keep her safe and out of the way for a little while. We've had a leak, and no immediate luck with alternate contacts and places. I'm only calling because it is rather urgent," Dee said.

"Well, I suppose I could. I have the room, no one really knows I'm here, and I suppose it is kind of out of the way, but without being too isolated," she said.

"And we would pay you. A lot," Dee said.

"When you say a lot, what do you mean," she asked.

"I'm authorized to pay five thousand dollars a day for up to ten days," Dee said in a serious voice.

That would cover the cost of a pickup truck. In fact, it could almost get her a new one. That made the offer very tempting. How much of a problem could it be having a woman stay as a guest for a week or so. It would even give her a chance to test out her bed and breakfast skills. The guest may even help out around the cottage.

Ophelia knew the drill of how the arrangements would work. Stella would need to stay out of sight and out of contact with the outside world. And Ophelia would keep her, most of the time, under observation. That wouldn't be too hard, it's not like she needed to go out much anyway, she'd already got most of the supplies she needed from town.

"Sure," she said. "For that kind of money I'd babysit her whole family," Ophelia said jokingly.

"Well actually, it's her family that we are hiding her from," Dee said.

"Oh, OK, bad joke. So how is she getting here?" Ophelia asked.

"I know this is going to sound rather clandestine, but we were hoping we could meet you somewhere for a change over tomorrow night. We were thinking somewhere halfway," Dee said.

"Do you mean somewhere halfway between Brisbane and Applethorpe?" she asked.

"Yes. There is a place on the Cunningham Highway called Arutula. We can do the changeover near the 24-hour service station around 10pm tomorrow night. From your direction, there is a road on the left just before the service station called Carter Road. It is an unpaved and unlight track. Just pull into there and our guys will find you and do the changeover. These guys are professionals, so there shouldn't be any risk of them being followed, especially out there at nighttime I'm sure they'd spot a tail," Dee assured.

"It sounds a lot like spies and espionage," she said.

"We wouldn't ask if it wasn't important. I know we can trust you to keep a low profile and make sure she stays safe," Dee said.

"I suppose I should ask, this Stella person, she is doing this willingly. I mean, it's not like I'm holding her as a prisoner, or against her will. She won't try to escape or anything?" Ophelia asked.

"No, no, not at all. She is scared and in hiding. She will do whatever you tell her is in her best interests. So no, she won't try to escape, or be any trouble for you at all," Dee assured her.

"Will you be there tomorrow night?" she asked.

"No, it will just be two guys and Stella," Dee said.

Well, this was certainly an interesting turn of events. The money was going to come in very handy, and a new face in the cottage that could keep her company and maybe help out, that sounded positive. This news certainly took her mind off the incident with Francesca, and it even distracted her from thinking about Trey, so it was already paying dividends.

CHAPTER 7

The following morning Ophelia baked two New York-style cheesecakes, and then, figuring that there would be two of them at the cottage for at least a week, she did another supply-run into town. She put one of the cheesecakes into the refrigerator, and the other she would take to the lodge. Maybe Francesca would be in a better mood and accept her gift with grace this time around.

Unfortunately, it was not to be. Like before she was treated like a lowly delivery driver who had distracted Francesca from her busy schedule. Yet Ophelia was amazed to see how Francesca could change her behavior, therefore outward appearance, on a dime. A guest would approach, and she would be sweet and helpful, and then she would turn back to Ophelia with cold indifference. Maybe that was why Trey and Francesca were business partners; he was everything that she was not, and vice versa.

It would take Ophelia one and half hours to reach the agreed meeting point to collect Stella. She decided to give herself another fifteen minutes in case there were roadworks, or some other delay. As usual it was cold and frosty, and because it was a new moon, it was dark. It was always risky driving these country roads at night. Most of the trucks took different routes, and most people had finished their commutes and were home, so it was a lonely drive.

There was also the risk of hitting kangaroos and other wildlife, and then being stranded on the side of the road, alone in the cold and dark for hours. And in some places, there was black ice. Especially on the winding mountain sections where water seeped across the surface of the road and then froze. This could be deadly the sharp downhill curves, and when she saw a warning sign, she slowed right down. There would be no one behind her, so no one to annoy. Thus, she carefully made her way down from the high country, eyes peeled and fully alert.

Arriving fifteen minutes early, she pulled into Carter Road. The bright lights from the service station were just ahead, down the highway, but she thought better of it than to go there first, even though she had the time and could have done with a coffee. There must have been a reason why they didn't want to meet her there. It was probably due to the surveillance cameras that covered every angle on the property. This secret mission was both exciting and scary at the same time.

She sat in the car, in the dark, parked under a

tree. After about 5 minutes, in the rear-view mirror, she could see a figure walking toward her. She watched it get closer, walk past the car, and then continue down the track that was Carter Road. It was either a local, or it was someone scouting to see if she was there. However, the way they were rugged up suggested they were a local.

She imagined the agents dropping Stella off would be wearing black suits, or in some way be recognizable as secret agents. They would not be wearing beanies and lumberjack coats like the person who had just walked past. Then she thought to herself, what if he was watching her, maybe wanting to steal the car or something. She checked the doors were locked and then turned on her parking lights. She wanted people to know that the vehicle wasn't abandoned, less they get ideas about breaking into it or steeling the wheels.

It was 10:15pm when a car pulled into her road, slowly drove past, continued some distance down the track and then turned around. It then drove back toward her with its headlights shining, allowing a full view of her sitting behind the steering wheel. It pulled up next to her and the driver wound down his window. When she did the same, he asked, "What is your name?"

"Ophelia," she said.

That must have been the 'password' because only then did they turned off their lights, and the front passenger and backdoor opened; no light came on in the car. A man went to their trunk and got out a suitcase, and then walked with a lady over to Ophelia's car. She unlocked the doors and boot. The lady got into the back seat, and the man put the suitcase in her boot.

The driver then said to Ophelia, "You can go now," and that was it. No message, not pleasantries, just drive away, 'real natural like'.

She drove up the track and turned at the same spot that the others had. When she returned the men were still sitting in their car, in the dark, probably watching to see if anyone had followed, or was about to follow. She reached the main road with the other car close behind hers, but with its lights still turned off. She indicated and turned onto the main highway, just like any other traveler would do, and then headed toward home. The other car did not follow her, it just stayed at the intersection of Carter Road and watched. In short time the lights from the roadhouse and town disappeared, and they were back on the dark dangerous road, winding their way back up into the mountains.

The woman in the back seat, Stella, had not spoken. She wore a scarf over her head, large dark glasses, and a trench coat. The outfit was a bit absurd but probably necessary when she travelled through the city. She really did look like she was playing a role in a spy movie, or impersonating Jacqueline Onassis incognito. Ophelia finally introduced herself,

"Hello, I'm Ophelia, and I presume you are Stella?" she enquired.

"Yes, I am Stella," the woman said.

Her accent was strong and most likely Italian. Right from her first words Ophelia got the impression that she did not want to talk. That was fine, she was probably stressed and scared. There was obviously some serious stuff she was involved with, and as is so often the case, the less someone knew about it the better. Ophelia asked if the temperature was OK for her, and Stella curtly replied, "It is fine."

They only spoke one more time during the journey when they approached another 24-hour service station and Ophelia asked if she needed to stop to use the rest room or buy anything. Stella replied, "No thank you, just keep driving."

It was near midnight when they arrived back at the cottage. Under the light of the porch Ophelia got the suitcase out of the boot and then warned Stella about the possibility of ice on the cobblestone path. The cottage was warm, and still had the aroma of cooking, as she barricaded them both inside. Heavy curtains were pulled across all the windows, and with the porch light turned off, the cottage disappeared into the night.

Finally, Stella removed her glasses, scarf, and trench coat, and for the first time Ophelia could get a good look at her. She was a very attractive woman with porcelain skin, perfect features, and long black wavey hair. She wore lots of makeup, in a way that made her old-world glamorous, as if she was in a Federico Fellini movie from the 1960s. She was wearing a black dress with a shawl and heals, as if she had just come from a fancy dinner or awards ceremony. How peculiar, it is not what she had expected, this woman looked strong, confident, and powerful. Ophelia had expected some mousey timid mother-type that had the look of a battered wife or drug addict. The cottage had stone floors with rugs. Stella power clicked as she walked on the stone, and then went stealth as she crossed the rugs.

"Would you like a cup of tea or coffee? The water is already hot," Ophelia enquired.

"Yes, tea please. I will take it in my room," she said.

"Of course, please follow me," Ophelia said as she lugged the suitcase up the stairs. She could not imagine Stella doing such a job. Not with what she was wearing or with those fingernails. And anyway, she probably always had a man to do such things, or some busboy in the service of her mafia-boss husband.

Stella's room was clean and comfortable, with a single bed and simple antique furnishings. She really did make the room. With its stone walls and rustic charm, it could have been a scene from Marsala Sicily. Ophelia left her to unpack and went downstairs to make the tea. While she was in the kitchen, she also made a simple antipasto that included some of her fresh cheese on savory warmed biscotti. By the time she had returned Sella was sitting up in bed. She had removed her makeup and changed; a task Ophelia could never have achieved in such a short space of time. Stella must have been a very organized and no-nonsense type of person, and well-practiced in the fashion arts. It was either that, or she wasn't really human, but instead some creature from Venus. Ophelia placed the tea and plater on the bedside table, bid Stella goodnight, and closed the door.

Ophelia liked having the fire burning in her bedroom, so she spent a few minutes getting it started. Silently she crept up and down the stairs getting kindling and wood, and then a warm mug of milk and some of the biscotti. She still had lots of milk to get through so this would probably become a ritual. It had been a long day, yet with all the excitement and intrigue she did not feel like sleeping. Instead, she sat up in bed with a book. In the silence she could hear Stella's voice. It was very faint, but it could not be anything else. She presumed that she was talking on a telephone. Yet, it struck her as rather odd. The point of disappearing was to cut communication with the outside world. Then she assured herself that Stella must have been briefed as to what she should or should not do, surely. Ophelia only read for thirty minutes before sleep took over.

Every morning of the previous week Ophelia had been up and working before the sun had risen. Today she slept in, and when she woke and opened the curtains, the sun was up, and the frost was almost gone. She dressed, opened her door, and looked toward the room where Stella was staying. The door was open and so she poked her head in. The room was tidy, the bed was made, but Stella was not there. Then she heard a noise downstairs, a clanging of pots and cutlery coming from the kitchen.

She went downstairs to find Stella busying herself at the woodstove. She must have re-started the fire and was now cooking scrambled eggs. There was also cottage cheese on toast, fried tomatoes, mushrooms, and asparagus. She was making enough for both of them, and two plates had been set at the table.

"Buongiorno a te," Stella said in a cheerful voice. "I hope you don't mind but I was much hungry. I have made la prima colazione for you and me."

This was quite a different person from last night. Yet still she wore an expensive dress, jewelry, and makeup, all protected by Ophelia's apron. Stella looked the epitome of a 'trad-wife' from the 1950s. Oh that breakfast looked and smelt good, with that added flavor that comes when someone else has cooked it for you. There was also a pot of hot coffee on the stove. Stella asked her how she took it, and then made it accordingly. Ophelia saw that Stella took it black and bitter; of course she did.

They sat at the table and ate breakfast together. Stella asked many questions about the farm and Ophelia's plans to develop it and turn a profit. Indeed, almost all the conversation was about Ophelia and the farm. None of it was about Stella, not even where she came from or how long she had been in Australia. Ophelia figured that if Stella wanted to keep it a secret, then that was fine with her. She did however say that the cottage, and the kitchen, reminded her of when she would stay with her nonna, grandmother, as a child. And how she loved cooking on the woodstove and using fresh farm grown ingredients.

She reminisced, "Oh, the tomatoes, such beautiful fresh tomatoes. Not like in the shops here. They are not the same here."

After breakfast and the morning thaw, they went for a walk around the property. Although there was still a chill in the air, the sun warmed what it touched. Stella was full of ideas of what could be grown, including fruit trees, vegetables, and herbs. She would point to a spot and say, "You must plant this here, and over there", with animated enthusiasm.

They weaved their way between the cows, that had decided that they liked Ophelia's pasture better than that on the diary side of the fence, all the way to the dry-stone wall that delineated the road frontage.

Ophelia noticed that each time a car drove past, which wasn't very often, Stella would turn her face away from the road so as not to be recognized. She had not thought to put her large sunglasses on, not expecting to walk all the way up to the road, but she did wear a large sun hat. Ophelia was a bit bemused as to how it had been packed into the suitcase and yet appeared uncrumpled. It must have been based on some of that advanced Venusian technology.

They strolled back down to the cottage and sat on the iron garden setting. It was a pleasant way to spend the morning, and it really stimulated ideas in Ophelia's mind about how she could run a guest house. Of course, not everyone would be as courteous and affable as Stella, and really, she would be better to put people in a renovated barn, rather than in the cottage. But still, possibilities abounded.

The phone rang and it was Dee.

"Hello, Ophelia, how is everything going?" she asked.

"Hello, Dee, yes, it's all good. We are just sitting outside in the sun chatting... No we are not up near the road...yes, I'll be staying at home... sure I'll put her on," Ophelia said.

Stella took the phone and then walked some distance away so she could talk to Dee in private. Ophelia could not make out what was being said, but whatever it was, Stella's mood became serious. At times she raised her voice, and this was accompanied by hand gestures flailing in air. It seemed that Stella was complex and had at least two personalities, and possibly many more.

CHAPTER 8

Each time Ophelia had dropped produce off at the lodge she included her phone number. A text came through from Francesca. She was ordering two more New York baked cheesecakes, and two-dozen buttermilk scones. Ophelia had never mentioned scones, and she had never actually made scones, but she certainly had lots of buttermilk that she needed to use up, so she would give it a try.

When she mentioned the order, Stella said, "This will not be a problem. I know the recipe for the scone. They will be golden and fluffy every time."

Ophelia sent a text back to Francesca saying that they would be made fresh and delivered by noon. The two of them got busy in the kitchen, making rapid progress, and when they were finished, fresh lavender was laid over the warm scones before they were wrapped in white linen.

Ophelia loaded everything into the car, and before driving away, assured Stella she would only be gone for thirty minutes. She had put a lock on the gate now that Stella was hiding out at the cottage. So, each time she went through, she had to find the keys and perform a routine. One day, if she could afford it, she would get an automatic gate, the type that has a keypad for putting in a secret pin number.

When Ophelia arrived at the lodge she saw Trey's pickup truck in the car park. 'Oh good', she thought, 'he must be back from his business trip'. She carried in the fragrant cheesecakes and the scones. Francesca was at the reception giving instructions to a younger employee. She was being rather strict and behaved in a similar way to how she treated her. Ophelia stood there being ignored so decided to put the baked goods in the area where she had put the other produce on the previous occasions.

Finally, Francesca acknowledged her existence and without a hello or thank you said, "I will need your bank details so we can pay you. I have worked out a price that I think is acceptable and will do the transfer in seven days. Oh, and from now on you will have to provide me with a proper tax invoice."

Francesca then handed Ophelia a printed sheet of paper that had a list of the products that they were interested in purchasing, and the prices they were prepared to pay. It was very presumptuous, and according to her experience of business, completely backwards. Then again, so many businesses are like this now. On the surface they seem honorable and ethical but dig deeper and you find they are deceitful greedy capitalists, underpaying and exploiting workers and suppliers. This was the impression Ophelia was getting of Francesca, and she was hoping that Trey was not cast from the same mold.

She took the price list and then asked, "Is Trey around; would I be able to see him?"

"No, I'm sorry he is not available," Francesca said.

The junior employee looked up at Ophelia but said nothing. Based on the employee's expression, it was obvious Francesca was lying.

"Oh, OK. Well could you please tell him that I was here," she said.

"Sure, I'll tell him, and we'll contact you if we need to place another order," she said without even looking up.

How rude Ophelia thought. The other employee smiled at her, a genuine smile, and wished her a good day. Of course, she knew Trey was here. Should she look around and maybe run into him, quite by accident? No, she couldn't, she had to get back to the cottage. She told Stella she would be gone for no more than thirty minutes, Damn. She hadn't even given Trey her phone number, but it was on all the stuff she delivered, so surely, he would call or text soon. Then again, knowing what she did of Francesca, then probably all of her labels had been peeled off and tossed in the rubbish.

When she arrived back at the cottage there was

a delivery van parked at the locked gate. The driver was on the phone calling his boss and asking what to do. It was lucky she caught him just before he drove back to the depot with her clothes and belongings. She unlocked the gate, and he helped her drag it open. By the time they got down to the house Stella had retreated to her room and closed the door. She obviously knew the drill and hid when anyone approached.

It was good to get the rest of her belongings. There were now pictures for the walls, a wider range of clothes to wear, and various items for the kitchen and bathroom. After the van left and the gate was locked, Stella helped her unpack and decorate. They were getting along well, even though Stella's former life, and current circumstances, remained a mystery. For all Ophelia knew Stella could have been a crime boss turned informant, or maybe even accused of murder. She had no idea, but then again who really knows anyone. But for now, they were getting along, and she trusted the person that she was with today.

Sometimes, in the dark, cows can make a lot of noise. It can be unnerving when it sounds like a cough or a stranger tripping over something in the dark. As they sat in the lounge room they heard such noises outside. Yet they dare not turn on the porch light, look through the windows, or investigate. All they could do was dim the inside lights and remain quiet until the noise and the fear subsided. Then they heard what sounded like footsteps on the cobblestones. Surely, a cow couldn't sound like that, a steady clip clop that got louder and louder. Then there was a knock on the door.

They both froze, and then Ophelia whispered, "Quick go up to your room and close the door. I'll see who it is."

From the first day Ophelia moved in she had kept an old axe handle, that she had found in the barn, next to the front door. She referred to it as her welcome stick.

Once Stella was upstairs, she picked it up and said through the door, "Who is it?"

"Ophelia, its Trey. I'm sorry if I scared you, again," he said.

She turned on the porch light and then peeped out through the curtains. She knew it was him by his voice, but still she wanted to check with her eyes. There he stood, looking rugged and handsome. A wave of relief washed over her, for more than one reason. It wasn't just that he was friend rather than foe, but also that it was a return to the dynamics and feelings of the previous week. Yes, now they could pick up where they left off, which was kind of, um, she wasn't sure. Oh, that's right, ecstatic, confused, jealous, insecure, and all with butterflies in her stomach. Yes, she was definitely coming down with something.

She had mentioned to Dee, and to Stella, that she had a friend called Trey who may come over to visit. She told them that she trusted him, although in both instances they reminded her that she had only known him for just over a week. However, she reminded them that they had met before there was any knowledge of Stella, or discussion of her staying at Lavender Cottage. She opened the door and invited him in.

His first comment was about the locked gate. He had to park his pickup up at the road and walk down the driveway in the dark. And he added that the cattle weren't too pleased with his presence. His second comment related to the axe handle she was still holding, and enquired whether that was intended for him, or if she was expecting other guests.

She laughed and said, "I thought it might be you knocking on the door, so I was getting ready."

"Nice, remind me not to get on your bad side," he said with feigned concern.

She closed the door and said, "I have a lady staying with me for a few days and she is a bit nervous. I'll introduce you if she comes downstairs, but please do me a favor and don't ask her about herself. She would rather keep that private."

"Sure. I don't understand, but hey, it's not my business, so whatever you say," he said with a shrug.

They sat in the kitchen and Ophelia made

two hot chocolates and asked him about his trip. Apparently, he had returned Sunday evening and had been at the lodge doing various odd jobs and maintenance. Thus, as she had suspected, Francesca had lied about his availability.

Then she asked, "So, what did you think of the Lavender Cottage products?"

"Oh," he said with surprise. "What products?"

There were several ways she could navigate this, and honesty won out. To hell with Francesca, she wasn't going to cover for her, or soften the blow. She would just tell it how it was and any conflict that may occur between Trey and Francesca was neither her doing or responsibility.

Ophelia described the deliveries of cheeses, butter, yoghurt, cake, and scones. She even described how it had been packaged and then took some out of the refrigerator to show him. He asked if he could try some while he was there, and she obliged. She even had some scones left, so warmed one up and put on some butter. It was still fresh from that day, and he liked it very much. He liked everything and even suggested she started baking biscuits to go with her hot chocolates.

He noticed that her phone number was on the packaging and asked if he could put it into his phone. Of course, she said yes, and then he texted her so that she now had his number.

He was genuinely surprised and said, "I'm baffled as to why Francesca never mentioned this," then said. "I suppose it must have slipped her mind."

Ophelia never mentioned that she had asked after him and was told he was unavailable. She didn't want to come across as petty. What was important is that Trey knew everything now, that they had shared phone numbers, and that he was here with her on the 'almost' first opportunity that he got.

They heard the clipping of heals as Stella came down the stairs and to the kitchen. There she stood in the doorway, poised and looking magnificent. Ophelia could have sworn that she had specially done her hair and make-up since Trey had arrived. She could not deduce if Stella was married, given that she had rings on all of her fingers, and yet none of them looked like any wedding band she had ever seen. Nothing was a plain band of gold, instead everything sparkled in every color.

Trey stood and greeted her like a gentleman, and then waited for her to sit before seating himself. That wave of panic washed over Ophelia again. Surely, Stella wasn't trying to seduce Trey? Stella's eyes widened and she leaned in toward him as she asked questions, in what had changed from a strong Mediterranean accent to romantic Latin. Maybe it was she who was the Godmother; Femme Fatale; the Vamp.

And Stella laughed, which only encouraged Trey

more, sometimes laughing so heartily that she had to touch his arm. This woman was good. She didn't need Trey; she could have any man she set her piecing dark eyes upon. So, what was she doing other than just sharpening her knife on Trey's ego? No wonder she needed to be hidden away, but the real question was for the safety of whom?

Ophelia reassured herself that Trey was equally skilled with women and accustomed to being fawned upon and flattered. For him there would have been easier marks than the mysterious Stella. Ophelia had witnessed as much the other night in the pub. And he did regularly look at her and draw her back into the conversation. Surely, he wasn't so dumb as to not know what was being played out here around the kitchen table.

Of course, Ophelia had only spoken of Trey as a friend, and never confided to Stella that she was beginning to have romantic feelings toward him. But then again, neither had she admitted anything like this to herself. Ophelia was not the type of person that made bold moves, or even the first move. And she had never been very good at reading the signs, and typically not recognizing them until they were pointed out by a friend, and often too late.

Was she missing the signs that Trey had, or was, sending out? It was so confusing. Was he just being friendly and helping her to settle into a new community and way of life, or did he try but had given up because he thought she was dead inside? Thinking that she was more concerned with making cheese and baking scones than in him. Was she going to become just the old lady down at Lavender Cottage where everyone got their herbs and dairy products?

After a couple of hours, Trey said, reluctantly, that he needed to leave. Stella followed him to the door, standing between Ophelia and him. She gave Trey a hug, a bit too sensual a hug in Ophelia's opinion, and then kissed him on both cheeks. It looked very Continental and natural for Stella to have done this. But oh my God, where the hell did this now leave her. If she just said goodnight, like she had done on all previous occasions, then what kind of a message would that send. However, if she gave him a hug, and a kiss, and it didn't match up to Stella's performance, then what would Trey think. Here he was getting a side-by-side comparison between two completely different women. How spoilt was he!

Ophelia stood frozen to the spot looking at him. She could not tell if there was longing in her eyes, or just a blank expression. What did he see? It was not something that she had trained for. As he stepped toward her, was he going to put her out of her misery or compound it? She looked at his hand to see if he was going to offer it in a handshake. That would have been death. The hand began to move toward her, but it kept moving until both arms were around her. At that moment she could have just collapsed and have him hold her full weight. Then he kissed her on each cheek, just like Stella had done to him. She didn't want him to pull away, and she actually, really, physically, did pull him in closer and tighter. It was not a conscious thing; it was as if someone else took control of her body. Someone else that had been living inside her and only showed up in her dreams.

And then it was over. Trey's arms fell to his sides, and he stepped back. She had to let go before it began to look obvious. Had he even noticed, or maybe this is what everyone did? Was it at least as good as Stella's embrace? He said he would be in touch and then headed out into the cold. Ophelia wanted to walk with him to his pickup truck, but that would have just been too obvious. And anyway, Stella may have invited herself, high heels and all, and maybe needed to be carried. That would not do. No, it was best to finish the evening like this. It was progress, small steps by most people's measure, but giant leaps for her. He came, he saw, he conquered, innocently and all without trying.

CHAPTER 9

Ophelia could see the dairy in the distance. She put on her gumboots and began to walk across the paddocks to see if Reggie was there. Given that she now had Stella to feed and was supplying more to the lodge than originally expected, she wanted to put in an order for another delivery of milk, and hopefully some more eggs. She carried a basket that had some of her produce, including freshly baked scones. As usual, it was a cold clear morning and she expected that the dairy workers would have good appetites. Milking had finished and the cows were heading back out across the fields, with many heading toward her property. The workers would be doing the clean-up and would appreciate something for their morning break.

It didn't cross her mind until she had climbed through a couple of fences that there may be a bull in one of the paddocks. She could not see anything that looked large and menacing, but she kept her wits about her all the same. When she reached the dairy she could see several people working, but no one paid her any attention. Then she saw a doorway with a sign above it that said 'Office', so that was where she headed. Through a window she could see Reggie sitting at his desk working on a computer. She knocked on the door and then opened it.

He remembered her name, where she was from, and seemed pleased to see her. He asked how she got on with the milk and eggs, and she told him all about it. Excitedly she placed the basket on his desk and opened up the cloth. He was very thankful that she had brough some of the produce back for them at the dairy. He said the workers would be finishing up the morning shift shortly and returning to the lunchroom. He was sure that the whole basket would disappear within a few minutes of being discovered. This pleased her greatly.

She then asked if she could have another delivery of milk, and if there were any eggs then she would take them as well. Reggie assured her that they still had a milk glut, and she could have as much as she wanted. She told him that the same size delivery as last time would be more than adequate. She also informed him that there was now a lock on the front gate and wondered whether they were able to do the delivery through the back gate that the cows were using. He said that it would not be a problem and that the milk and eggs would be at her back door tomorrow morning, along with her basket and linen cloth. She thanked him and then asked if there were any bulls in the paddocks, to which he said no, but it was always wise to ask.

It was a relaxing fifteen-minute walk in the sun

across the green pasture. Some parts were a bit boggy from natural seeps, and of course there was cow manure everywhere that had to be avoided. Reggie had told her that she could take as much manure as she wanted for her garden. That was something she hadn't yet organized. She needed to start thinking about a garden so it could be ready for planting in the spring.

She also wanted to get fruit trees, as Stella had suggested. Lots of fruit was grown in the region, and she could probably trade some of her produce for apples, pears, and the like, but still she was fond of having some of her own trees. Maybe she could get some rare or heirloom types that weren't normally available? It would certainly fit with the historic character of Lavender Cottage.

She walked down a gentle slope affording her a view of her property and the cottage. She could see all the way up to the dry-stone wall at the front, and the heavy iron gate. It was when looking toward the front that she noticed a vehicle parked on the side of the road. It was a plain white commercial van. The type that would be used for parcel deliveries or perhaps by a tradesperson. It was too far for her to see anyone inside, and even if she were closer, they would likely be concealed by its dark tinted windows.

Normally, one would not pay much attention to such a vehicle. However, given that there was really no logical reason for anyone to be parked there, and the fact that Stella was hiding out in the cottage, it piqued her interest. Instead of going through the gate onto her own property, she continued down the center of the dairy paddock and then through the fence and onto the road. If no one knew any better, they would have thought she was coming from the dairy, likely being one of the employees.

As she approached the van from behind, she covertly took a photograph of its numberplate. Before she got level with the driver's window the engine started, and it began to drive away. It took off slowly and in a completely normal fashion, rather than if it were panicked and trying to escape. She watched as it drove about half a kilometer up the road and then pulled off to the side and stopped again. Maybe it really was a parcel delivery van, and the driver was trying to find an address. Sometimes it was difficult on these poorly signposted and numbered country roads.

Still, she decided to keep up the charade just in case they were watching her. So, she continued on for about one hundred meters past her gate and then turned into the winery that bordered the other side of her property. It was the first time that she had been in there, and if she continued, it would have been a considerable downhill walk to the cellar door and barrel sheds. However, she decided that once she passed out of view from the van, she would cut back across to her own property. She had been away from the cottage about twice as long as she had told Sella she would be, so she needed to get back and check on her. Perhaps, tomorrow or later in the week she could tour the winery. Maybe she could ask Trey if he would like to accompany her. Just him and her. She would convince Stella that it would be too dangerous for her to be seen in public, even if it was only next door.

The vines in winter looked bleak as they rested till spring. Pruned back to almost stumps the rows looked like a military cemetery commemorating a long-ago battle, maybe in France during the First World War. In the most beautiful, lush green setting, one could imagine the vibrant poppies and daisies stretching for the sun amongst the sticks naming the young men that fell. 'Fell'. What a soft way to say, 'died a horrible death'. She was sensitive to war and loss; her grandfather had been killed fighting for his country when he was younger than she was now. Her grandmother never re-married, such was her grief. Perhaps they were once again together again in the version of heaven that they had believed in.

There was a large oak tree that grew on the fence line between the properties. Its branches hung low and obscured a direct view between the winery buildings and Lavender Cottage. It must have been planted when the farm was first established around 160 years ago. The stone cottage wasn't built at that time. Instead there was a wooden hut, but that had long ago succumbed to the elements. She did, however, have a picture of the original property, provided by the estate agent, and then another picture when the stone cottage was first built in the 1880s.

The dry leaves crunched underfoot as she negotiated the fence and then made her way to the cottage. There was no sign of Stella, which was good. She had been instructed not to stand out in front of the cottage, only to go outside at the back so she would not be seen from the road. Even the curtains remained three quarters drawn such that they could see out, but no one could see in.

She walked to the back of the cottage. Stella was hanging washing upon the line. It was the most domesticated Ophelia had ever seen her. She did have a modern washing machine and drier in an annex laundry room, however, many of Stella's clothes were too delicate for either the washer or the drier. Before sunset all of the washing would need to come in and be draped over wooden drying racks in front of the fires. It was the only way to dry things properly during the winter months.

Stella seemed to be in a good mood. Perhaps doing chores suited her. She said, "It's been years since I've washed and hung out clothes, but I suppose like riding a bike, it's not something that you forget."

"You must have lived a privileged life if you always had your clothes washed for you," Ophelia said.

"Oh, it's more a case of different circumstances in different places. In some countries the labor is so cheap, servants do everything. In Australia it's not so cheap or normal, so in that case it is what you would call privileged," Stella said as she reflected on a mysterious past.

"So how long have you been in Australia?" Ophelia asked.

"Not long, maybe six months, before that Colombia for a couple of years, and then before that, different countries in Europe," Stella said.

"Wow, that's a lot of different places to call home," she exclaimed.

"I wouldn't have called any of them home, they were just places where I had to live. But even then, there was still lots of travelling and living out of a suitcase. No, home was once Salerno Italy," she said with a distant look.

"Where is that in Italy?" Ophelia asked.

"It's down below Naples, on the Amalfi Coast, do you know where?" Stella asked.

"Yes, I know where Naples is, and I have seen pictures and movies about the Amalfi Coast. It must have been really lovely there. So that is where you grew up?" she asked.

"Yes, I was there until I was fifteen. We would hang the washing out like this, and it would be dry within a few hours. All the old ladies did the washing in the morning and by lunch they would bring it in."

"What did your father do?" Ophelia enquired.

"He was a 'scalpellino', what you call a stone mason. He would cut stone and build with it. He was very artistic and well regarded. I'm sure he would have admired your stone cottage," she said as she looked back at the old building.

"It is a long way from Italy to South America and then to Australia. Did you travel with your family or was it for work or something?" she asked.

"I left home when I was fifteen and then I married young. I've had a few husbands but some of them have died. This is all I can say," she said rather abruptly.

"Oh, I'm sorry to hear about your losses, that must have been hard," Ophelia said with genuine sympathy.

But Stella seemed to have suffered no injury, and casually said, "It is OK. Stupid and careless things happen. It is important that I am alive, and my children are alive."

"Oh, so you have children. That is always a comfort. Where are they now?" Ophelia asked.

"I have a son and a daughter. They are grown up and have left home. I am not sure where they are now," Stella said in a dispassionate way.

By Ophelia's reckoning that would make Stella's age somewhere around late thirties or early forties. She certainly looked young for her age and had maintained a model's figure.

"So, you don't keep in touch? That is a shame," she said.

"Oh, I see them and hear from them, but just not for the past six months when here in Australia," she said.

"Why is that?" Ophelia asked but was not expecting a clear or straight answer.

"I cannot tell you this. Not at this time," Stella said rather abruptly.

By this time, she had finished hanging out the clothes and was returning to the cottage.

She turned to Ophelia and said, "I have made the lunch, and you can take it now."

Ophelia followed her inside. On the kitchen table was some crusty bread, a spread of salad, olives, cheese, and cold meat. For someone who appeared to have lived a privileged life, Stella still seemed to know her way around a kitchen, and how to present a lovely meal.

They sat, ate, and talked, although none of the conversation dealt with Stella's past or current circumstances. It seemed the door was now closed on that topic. Perhaps tomorrow it may get opened again. For the rest of the afternoon Ophelia busied herself stripping paint off one of the antique chairs. They were solid enough but had been painted so many times over the years that the layers were now cracked and chipped. Methodically she would take them back to wood and then relacquer them, one chair at a time, and then afterward the table so they all matched.

Stella sat in a lounge chair, reading a book and sometimes looking out through the partially open curtain. Ophelia was an avid reader and her book collection had arrived with the delivery van. Stella rummaged through the boxes of books until she found something of interest. Of all the books and genres, she could have chosen from, she selected a murder mystery. Did that say something about her character and her past or was it purely for the same reasons that Ophelia had bought the book. Simply because there was a good illustration on the cover, and an interesting blurb.

CHAPTER 10

The cows were restless, interrupting the otherwise peaceful evening. Stella must have been a very patient person to wait out her time as she did. Ophelia was itching to get out. Someway, somehow, she wanted an excuse to see Trey. They would be getting another delivery of milk in the morning. At least that would give her an excuse to trek down to the lodge and ply her produce.

She hadn't received an order from Francesca, so instead she would text Trey, real casual like, and say that she had some freshly made stuff and ask if he was interested in a delivery. She was sure he would say yes, and then she could suggest that he meet her when she arrived. It would require finesse and perfect timing. She would out-fox Francesca this time. 'Look out for him', he had said. Ha, she'd see about that.

There was a sound outside, as if a bucket had been kicked over. They both looked at each other and then Ophelia got up and turned the lights off until only the small lamp in the lounge room remained on. She went upstairs and peeped out though the curtains, first to the front of the house and then to the rear. She could not see anything. There was a thick fog tonight which made it extra dark and claustrophobic.

The doors were old and solid, and the locks were new and sturdy. Unfortunately, the same could not be said about the windows. They were just timber with single pane glass. The window frame locks could be forced, and the glass could be easily broken. Of course, they would hear if anyone attempted to get in through a window, but that was different from stopping them. What would they do if someone came through a window? And if intruders were going to go to the effort of coming through a window, when they knew the women were home, then obviously the intruders had dangerous intentions. All she had was her old axe handle.

It wasn't like in the movies where she would be sitting and waiting in the dark with a loaded shotgun. Or even more fantastical, that she was an ex-military secret ops soldier ready and able to kick their butts. No, it was just her and Stella, and from what she deduced of the latter, she may have been quite capable of ordering a hit on a rival, but she didn't seem like the type to get her hands, or her Gucci, dirty by actually doing it herself.

They kept still and listened in the half-light. -Buzz- They both jolted with surprise. Ophelia's phone received a message. It was from Trey, and he was enquiring whether she was able to provide two-dozen scones for tomorrow morning, along with some butter and cream. And if she possibly had any homemade strawberry or other jams. The sounds outside, and in her imagination, ensured that she was wide awake, and would probably not fall asleep for hours.

She said to Stella, "Do you feel like making some scones? I've got an order for two-dozen, and they need to be delivered tomorrow morning."

"Sure," Stella said. "I'm not feeling sleepy either."

It seemed to shake them out of their paralyzing fear, as a distraction and getting on with it often does. They had enough ingredients to make the scones, and they could skim and whip cream from tomorrow morning's milk delivery. Amazingly, Ophelia also had an unopened jar of strawberry jam, although it was store bought. That was another thing that she wanted to produce at Lavender Cottage, being jams, chutneys, and preserved fruits. That old woodstove had opened more possibilities for her than she could have ever imagined before she first lit it.

They needed more wood for the fire. The pile in the kitchen was almost depleted so someone had to go outside to get it. The woodshed was on the other side of the back lawn, about thirty meters away and beyond the pitiful power of the rear porch light, and then there was the thick fog. One may as well be using a flashlight to walk a path through a graveyard on the moors. It was the perfect setting for The Hound of the Baskervilles.

Of course, the task fell to Ophelia. She took the wood basket in one hand, and in the other she held her phone as a torch. She made a mental note to buy a powerful flashlight next time she went shopping. Even better, get an electrician to wire up some decent lighting around the property.

She crept her way down the path as Stella stood on the rear porch watching. It was unclear what the logic was. Would it be that if one got attacked, then the other could get away? Then again, separating never seemed a good strategy in horror movies.

The fog was ridiculously thick, and as Ophelia approached the woodshed, she turned to see that the cottage was fully blurred. All she could see was a smudge of light where Stella should have been standing. She was almost at the end of the path when she was startled by a noise to the side of her. She quickly turned to see a black figure a few meters away. As she shone the light it moved, and eyes reflected back through the mist. Her heart was pounding, and she was about to drop the basket and run when she realized it was a cow. She gave out a nervous laugh and then kept walking until she reached the shed.

As she loaded the wood, she continued to look to the sides and behind her. Even though she knew there were only cows, her imagination could conjure so much more. There were no wolves or bears in Australia. The only thing apart from cows that she may see would be kangaroos. But still, there were people. They could be deadly, and then there were the creatures of myth and fantasy. The things that scared you as a child, and continued in your imagination when you are an adult.

She was almost back to the cottage when she saw another dark figure near the corner of the walls. The light and shadows played tricks. It was probably a cow, but it looked so much like a human. She shone the light toward it and it vanished, as if it had moved around the corner of the building. She lowered the light and looked again. This time there was nothing. She could put the basket down and go and investigate, alone in the dark and the mist, or she could convince herself it was just a cow, or a trick of the light. She elected for the later and hurried to the back door where Stella was faithfully waiting. When they got inside, she quickly locked the door and they warmed themselves by the woodstove.

Strangely, going outside and facing her fears, and convincing herself that every noise was a cow, settled her nerves. Not that she wanted to go outside again, but neither was she so jumpy. It seemed to also have the same effect on Stella. They spent the next few hours baking and preparing for tomorrow and were in bed before midnight. She was expecting the milk delivery to occur around 6.30am, just before sunrise, and so she set an alarm accordingly.

When Ophelia went outside in the morning, the milk and eggs had been delivered. However, there was something else this time. There were two large blue-grey pumpkins. 'How sweet', she thought. If she hadn't already baked the scones the night before she could have done a batch of pumpkin scones, maybe she would do that for the next order. It was something she could discuss with Trey. Another reason to meet with him.

She could see the tracks from the ATV that Reggie, or one of the dairy employees, had left when they did the delivery. There were also footprints in the frost that had cracked through the ice on a frozen puddle. She looked back to the corner of the house where she thought she had seen the shadowy figure the night before. She walked over and saw hoof marks from cattle, but there were also human footprints. She could not tell the difference between the first set she had seen, being those that were clearly made by the person doing the delivery, and now this new set. It was possible that the delivery person had walked around the corner to check where the right place was to drop the milk, but then again, the back porch was a pretty obvious place. She logged her suspicions and then returned to the task at hand.

Stella came down to the kitchen about an hour later, which was still in time to help out, and within a couple of hours the produce was prepared and loaded into the car. Stella remained at the cottage, even though she complained she was getting housebound and would have loved to come with her. Ophelia wondered if part of the reason was that she had mentioned she would try to talk to Trey.

Having arrived at the gate she got out to unlock it. It was then she noticed there were boot marks on the ground, on the outside of the property, as if someone had been walking near the gate. There were also other marks further along the roadside of the fence, and maybe, just maybe, there were marks where someone had climbed over the fence. It was difficult to tell and may have actually been caused by a cow. Again, she logged her suspicions and then got back into the car. She sent a text to Trey informing him that she was 15 minutes away. His reply was simply a smile emoji. It made her smile.

It was still foggy, but not as thick as it was during the night. She drove slowly down the track to the lodge just in case someone was coming the other way. When she arrived, Trey was standing in the carpark waiting for her. He was all rugged up against the cold and looked very huggable. He carried the basket for her as they went inside. It was a completely different reception than the cold indifference she had received from Francesca.

He led her through the 'staff only' doors and into the kitchen. There was a chef and kitchen hand on duty, and he introduced her to them. The chef immediately unwrapped the swaddled scones, beamed a smile at Ophelia and said, 'Perfecto'.

When she pulled out the fresh whipped cream, and the strawberry jam he said, "Yes, yes, yes, now this is what I'm talking about." He turned to Trey and said, "This is what I was wanting, food with that old country charm. You can tell it's been cooked in a woodstove and made with the freshest of ingredients."

Ophelia said, "I should think so, the milk used to make the cream only came out of the cows this morning. Although, I'm sorry the jam is store bought, I haven't started making jams yet, but it is in my plans."

The chef then asked, "What else can you do?"

"I got some pumpkins this morning, so I was going to make some pumpkin scones, maybe tomorrow. And I've got so much lavender that I was going to incorporate it into the products. You would have seen a little bit in previous things, so yeah, I'm planning on doing more," she said.

The chef turned to Trey and said, "We should take everything she makes. I know we can use it all, but even if we don't, we can send it home with guests in gift packs or something."

The four of them broke open a warm scone each, buttered, jammed, and creamed them, and then ate breakfast with fresh ground coffee. What a way to start the day.

Ophelia handed the invoice to Trey, and he

slipped it into a folder at reception.

He said, "That's Francesca's department. I assume you are happy with what she is paying you?"

"It will do for now, but it's early days, so I will need to review my costs in a month or so," she said.

"Just don't let her shortchange you. Just between you and me, I know she can be ruthless, so be sure to stand up for yourself," he said and then looked around as if checking she wasn't within earshot.

As they walked together back out to the car she asked, "You drive past my front gate a lot, don't you?"

"Yes, usually a couple of times a day," he said.

"Would you mind just keeping an eye out for a white van, or actually any vehicles that are parked near my property? It's probably nothing, but there was a van there yesterday, and it drove off as I walked up to it. And then at sometime during the night it looks like someone was standing near my gate and walking along the fence. Now, it is probably nothing, but just text me if you are driving past and see anything," she said.

"Sure. Would you want me to stop and ask what they are doing?" he suggested.

"No, I'd rather you didn't, just in case it's completely innocent and we start upsetting people. However, maybe you could take a picture or jot down their registration just in case we need to follow it up with the police," she said.

"Now you've got me worried. Are you scared there at night? Would you like me to come over and check on you tonight?"

Wow. Now how to get rid of Stella. A sleeping potion perhaps?

"That would be very sweet of you. Perhaps you could come over for dinner?" she said.

"I like the sound of that. You do the cooking and I'll bring the wine," he said with a smile.

"Deal. Is there anything you don't eat?" she asked.

"I'm from the country, I eat any and everything," he said.

"Then how does traditional roast lamb and vegetables sound, infused with my homegrown rosemary?" she asked.

"It sounds perfect. I can't wait. What time do you want me there?

"Maybe 6.30pm. Is that OK?" she asked.

"Perfect. Oh, and what do you drink?" he asked.

"Anything. I'll trust your judgement," she said.

He replied cheerfully, "Then wine it is."

He stood in the carpark and waved as she drove away, and continued to stand there until she rounded a corner and disappeared from sight.

She drove straight into town and stopped at the butchers.

"Your best leg of lamb please, a big one," she said.

Unfortunately, she couldn't avoid the reality

that it would be a dinner for three, rather than the preferred deuce. After the butchers she went to the hardware store and bought a high-powered flashlight. No more would she have cows sneaking up and scaring her in the middle of the night.

CHAPTER 11

It was mid-afternoon when Ophelia informed Stella that Trey would be coming that evening for dinner. Stella did not ask if Ophelia wanted some time alone with Trey. Instead, she said excitedly, "I must start to get ready," and then disappeared upstairs to her room.

This left Ophelia to gather firewood, clean downstairs, and to cook the meal. Thus, it didn't leave her much time to get herself ready. She didn't have the stylish clothes that Stella had and was guaranteed to wear. Instead, Ophelia dressed like a 'country gal', and she thought she looked rather cute, and more to the point, she thought it would be more to Trey's taste. But who really knew the minds of men; they are distracted by new and shiny things.

Ophelia had given Trey a key to the gate. It wasn't the same as a key to the house, obviously, but it was definitely a step in that direction. He arrived with a couple of minutes to spare and then sat in his car until the agreed time. How cute was that. He wore his smart casual country clothes, perfectly matching what Ophelia wore.

In contrast, and with consistency, Stella wore a dress. Black of course. It plunged embarrassingly low at the front and made it hard to concentrate on the pearls that graced her perfect neck. And just so they were not lonely, perfect pearls swung on vertical bars from each ear. They were as large as marbles and had the sheen of blued and burnished steel. Her hair was up; so much hair that defied gravity must have taken hours of work. How she could do it without the help of a hairdresser was beyond Ophelia's comprehension. Clip clop went her dangerously high heels on the stone floor.

She did not say 'Darling' with drama and flair when she greeted Trey, but she may as well have, when she did her grand entrance. Of course, she hugged him and kissed him on both cheeks. Maybe a bit longer than before and leaving a smudge of rose red lipstick. Ophelia gave him a hug after Stella was finished. Tactfully, she had a tissue and remained in his embrace while wiping off the lipstick that Stella had left. Removing her branding before it could set or have effect.

It was a good evening. The food was delicious and comforting. His choice of wine was fitting and probably quite expensive. He brought more than they could possibly drink and said that it would be the start of Ophelia's wine collection. She didn't really have many reasons to drink at home, but of course, in the future she may be doing more entertaining, both with Trey, and maybe with other guests.

It was a dark, cold, and misty night. The cows were up to their antics out in the paddock, and yet in the bright, warm, cottage they were boisterously oblivious. All of the drama and fear of the night before was forgotten. As sexist as it sounded, the women felt safe while a man was with them. Stella could really drink. She outdrank both of them, and the more she drank, the more charismatic and seductive she became, but still, she did not spill her secrets. Ophelia was silently frustrated that Stella could not keep her hands off of Trey, which actually made him more attractive to her. Yet, he seemed to take it all in his stride. He even winked at Ophelia as a sign of allegiance, rather than falling for Stella, on an occasion when Stella was being a bit too forward.

Soon Sella would crash. Surely, her system could not take any more alcohol, and indeed, did not. Within a short space of time, she went from dancing to almost staggering. She did not embarrass herself, but both Trey and Ophelia had to help her up the stairs and onto her bed. They removed her shoes, put the covers over her, and then left her to sleep it off. Perhaps the excess was a sign of the stress she was under. Maybe for the first time in a long time she felt safe enough to let go and to laugh and play the fool. No doubt she would have a hangover in the morning.

When they got back downstairs it seemed that

Stella had taken the party to bed with her. Now it was something different. The kitchen no longer seemed appropriate, and they retired to the lounge room, and were seated in two stately chairs that faced each other. As Thoreau alluded to in 'Walden', they now had enough distance, and ambiance, for their words, and their meanings, to mature as they journeyed the space between them, as if the words interacted with environment and time, like sailors seasoned with each exotic port of call.

For long periods, that would be uncomfortable for most people, and couples, they just sat and looked at each other. Yet, even that was as loud and meaningful as any utterance. Then a thought would come along, with no rhyme or reason, and there it was, presented for the other person to respond. It made no sense and yet perfect sense in that moment. 'How wonderful', she thought. Is this how a soul mate feels and behaves, and does it go on forever? Or is this as good as it gets, and everything afterwards will never live up to this moment? Should she be trying harder to immerse herself in it, to experience it to its fullest, imprinting it as deep and solidly in her memory as possible? Gobble up every bit so she can re-live it later when she is lost and lonely, when he is gone. Oh god, he will have to go soon, and then she will have to come back to Earth and once again live down here with mortals.

But it did last longer. He produced an interesting

bottle of something he called mastiha liqueur. It was a sweet digestif from Greece, apparently from just one island in the Aegean, and he said it would be a perfect way to end the evening. She would be the judge of that. It was very pleasant without being too powerful when sipped. Surely, he must be falling in love with her, what more could a girl do short of hog-tying him. Yet, still she could feel the conversation drifting toward 'kali-nihk-ta', a Greek goodnight.

And then he said it, "Well, I suppose I had better get going. I have an early start tomorrow," and he stood up to leave, put on his coat and made his way to the door.

In rapid fire she made small talk about her plans for tomorrow and the rest of the week, but nothing slowed his departure.

Then in a serious tone he said, "If you get scared, or anything bothers you, just send me a text message, and if I don't respond then call. I'm only fifteen minutes away."

She thought to suggest he was welcome to stay the night, but then thought better of it. The perceived threat and her level of fear just didn't warrant it; hence her true motives would be exposed. She did, however, edge in that direction by saying, "Are you sure you are sober enough to drive?"

"Yeah, I'm fine. I'm sure that both Stella and you drank more than me, especially Stella."

Oh yes, that's right, there was the body upstairs. Over the past hour she had completely forgotten that Stella existed, that anything existed apart from Trey and her. Oh dear, what to do, the door was getting opened and there was no lead from Stella with regard to acceptable and innocuous hugs and kisses. Thankfully, he took the lead and gave her a hug. She did not get the feeling that he was going to kiss her, so she sneaked one in on his neck. He was the better of the evening's digestifs.

Then it was too late, he was driving up the track toward the front gate. As he approached, she saw the lights of a car further down the road switch on and then it quietly drove away. It was down near the entrance to the winery and would have been obscured from Trey's sight. She could just make it out from the front porch.

Maybe it was nothing. It was not uncommon for vehicles to be driving in and out of the winery at all hours. Yet still there it was, coincidental, and travelling in a direction that took it away from the main road and town.

The cottage was quiet, and once again she could hear the night sounds. She went upstairs to check on Stella. She appeared as sleeping beauty, and Ophelia wondered what dreams were dreamt. Then she went back to the kitchen. While tidying she had a choice, she could micro-analyze Trey's every word and gesture throughout the evening, or she could concern herself with the feeling she was being watched.

She checked the downstairs doors and windows, and they were all locked. What more could she do? This paranoia hadn't existed before Stella came to stay, and she hoped that it would subside when she left. She did enjoy having Stella in the house, but she also knew that it was for a short time. Ophelia's life would take a different path than where Stella steered the boat, for both good and bad. Stella was like a hit of adrenaline, much could be achieved, but then she would wear off.

After checking on Stella one last time, Ophelia put an extra log on the fire in her bedroom and slipped under the covers. She kept her door open, in part to regulate heat, and more so to listen. Maybe it wasn't the best idea given that it took her a long time to fall asleep, with each creak of the cottage or thump of a cow jolting her awake. She would look over at the axe handle and then close her eyes.

Ophelia woke to the sound of a message arriving on her phone. It was much later in the morning than she would normally be getting out of bed. She could hear Stella was already up as pots banged in the kitchen. When she went downstairs Stella seemed bright and refreshed rather than hung over the rope like a sickly sailor.

"How are you feeling?" Ophelia asked.

"I am fine," she said. "I sleep well and now the coffee is good."

Maybe by getting drunk she had blotted out her troubles, whatever they may be, and finally she had a good night's sleep.

"And where is Trey?" Stella asked, as if it was a perfectly normal question. "I see he is not here."

"He left last night around 11pm," Ophelia replied.

"Oh...," Stella said. "You let him go? I see. He is just your friend. Maybe he has someone else, yes?"

"No, he doesn't have someone else, well not that I know about. He hasn't said anything," Ophelia said defensively but with a hint of alarm.

"But you do not know him well, just only one week, I think," Stella said, reminding Ophelia of her own mother.

"No, I'm sure he doesn't have a girlfriend or is pursuing anyone. He's not like... He would have said something," she said trying to convince herself.

"Then if you like, you take him. For a night, for a week, forever," Stella said in a very pragmatic and matter of fact way. It was the type of thing one would expect a psychopath to say. Indeed, she said it without even turning to look at her, as if it was just a common everyday occurrence and required no further explanation.

Had Ophelia been so transparent, and if she was, then why the hell had Stella been pawing Trey in her feline ways? She was only going to be staying at the cottage for a few more days, and then would return to whatever place and life she came from. And didn't she have a husband? It was all very murky. Then again, maybe it was her husband she was hiding from. Maybe he too was a psychopath. What a frightening thought. A family of vampires that used humans for sport.

Stella continued, "Or maybe you do not like or want him?"

"Yes, I do like him," was Ophelia's reflex. "I mean, we get along well, and I enjoy his company," but she did not admit out aloud the want.

"Then that is enough. Everything else will work with time and patience. And he is good looking, this is a benefit," she said, like a scientist explaining Newtonian physics.

Stella must have grown up in a very different world than herself. Such pragmatism: but then again, if you are as beautiful as she, then all one need do is pick the most agreeable candidate amongst a long line of suiters. Perhaps she had had so many husbands and lovers that romance became oh so passé. Or maybe she realized that life was short and fragile, and pouring everything into one person was foolish? Instead, small amounts of her soul were begrudgingly metered out, one fleeting fascination and dalliance at a time. Something always in reserve for the next squeeze, for a Trey, should one wander too close.

"I'm just taking it slow while I get to know him," Ophelia said.

"What is there to know? He is a man," Stella said mockingly. "They are the same. It is you who is unique, and you who makes the difference. You take him if you want, or you leave him."

Ophelia just laughed. Not because Stella had said anything amusing, but rather that she had not, and Ophelia had no clear thoughts or words to offer.

Then she stammered, "I... I... don't know..."

Stella waved her hand and said, "Piff, if you do not want him, then I will have him. He is there to be taken. You tell me yes or no and I respect this. It is your house and your friend, but I do not want this fruit to go to waste."

Ophelia sat stunned at the table. Stella left the room and went upstairs, perhaps to apply another layer of makeup. She really was quite the psychopath. The world and its people were just resources, or obstacles, on her search for gratification. Should she feel privileged and thankful that Stella had given her first dibs on Trey or was it just all bluster. Ophelia could follow the foolish romantic path and say to herself, I will let him choose. But what kind of fool would she be to leave her future to those odds? Would that not be tempting fate? A neurotypical person can't beat a psychopath on a level playing field.

Yet she had to give Trey credit, or she would be reducing her opinion of him down to Stella's level. Surely, he was more than just 'a man', as Stella had categorized him. For Ophelia, he was 'the man', and that meant he was not tempted by the likes of Stella, but instead attracted to the honestly and purity of herself. The cute 'country girl' who lived in Lavender Cottage and made scones and butter and other wholesome things. He would fall in love with her for the right reasons, and this would always trump the lust that the likes of Stella would try to cultivate.

Just to be sure, she would have to see him again, soon, and away from Stella. She texted him to ask if he was free for an hour or two, and could he drive her into town. The reply came back quickly. He would be free and could pick her up at noon. She waited at the gate for him to arrive, looking as sweet as she could surrounded by flowers and sunshine.

CHAPTER 12

As she waited, she walked both side of the road. There were fresh tire tracks in the damp earth, and more footprints around the gate and along the fence that could not be explained. It was concerning and a sound basis for paranoia, but still it was inconclusive.

Trey arrived on time. She liked that he was punctual. He was wearing a cowboy hat, and she really liked the look. She took it off his head and put it on herself.

He smiled and said, "Wow, that really suits you," so she continued to wear it because it pleased him, and that pleased her.

"So where are we off to?" he asked.

"I'm going to buy a pickup truck, and hopefully take it home today," she said.

"Oh well, then you will need to keep the hat to look the part," he said with a laugh. She got the impression that it was a serious offer. It was as good as if he had given her his football jacket in high school. It made her feel young and carefree.

"So, how did Stella pull up this morning?" he asked.

"She seemed absolutely fine. In fact, she was up before me," Ophelia said.

"She's a real live wire that one," he said.

Ophelia wasn't sure if that was a complement or a criticism. How could she enquire while still appearing to get his gist?

"Yes, she can drink and talk a lot. It was the first time I have seen that side of her," she said.

"So, she didn't want to come with us today?" he enquired.

"No, she wasn't interested in looking at cars and trucks," she said, but felt bad about not telling the truth. Stella was in fact itching to get out of the house but knew that she couldn't for safety reasons. And Stella would have probably like to have seen Trey when he came to pick her up, even if just to see a different face.

She wondered if she was overreacting and being mean by meeting Trey up at the gate. She convinced herself that if all is fair in love and war, then she was defending her interests, and perhaps also protecting Trey from Stella.

They drove past the old pickup truck for sale on the side of the road. Trey slowed down, and then they both looked at each other and at the same time said 'nah' and kept driving. They arrived at one of only two car yards in town and walked around to see what was on offer. Ophelia still wore Trey's cowboy hat and he seemed to like that. The new vehicles were out of her price range, and had long delivery times, so they concentrated on the used vehicle section.

There were some late model pickup trucks that had low milage and were in good condition. Some of them came with a range of accessories including bull-bars, spotlights, and aftermarket wheels. The prices were steep, but still within her budget. One vehicle in particular took her interest. When she posed next to it, Trey said she looked real 'Boss'.

It was a four-door pick-up with blacked out bars and accessories. The suspension had been lifted so it sat high on big chunky tires. She could visualize having Lavender Cottage painted down the side and maybe some purple decals. It was big, powerful, and perfect. They went for a test drive, and it took her a while to get used to the size. It wasn't quite as wide as Trey's vehicle, but it was taller and definitely looked more intimidating. Trey told her to drive down a side road that turned to dirt and climbed a hill. They stopped the vehicle on a steep rocky slope, and he showed her how to use the low range 4WD system. Then on another section of road he showed her how to use the recovery equipment, and they pulled the vehicle up the slope by its winch. This was fun and it made her feel empowered. She had to have it, and after signing some papers and transferring money, she was set to drive it home.

Trey followed her back to the cottage. Still wearing his hat, she jumped out, unlocked the gate, and then bumped at a reasonable speed down the driveway. Unlike her other car, it did not scrape or struggle on the uneven terrain. There was enough space in the shed to park it next to her other car, but only just enough room for it to fit under the roof beams. She put it to bed and locked it. Trey was standing nearby and said he couldn't hang around for very long because he had work to do. Still, she asked him if he wanted to come in, and he agreed to a cup of tea and a scone if she had any left. Indeed, she did. In fact, they were her very first attempt at pumpkin scones, a Queensland country staple, smeared with homemade butter. She encouraged him to have several and he willingly obliged.

Stella slinked down the stairs, prepared as always for gentlemen callers. She lit up and called out 'Trey', then came up behind him when he was seated at the table. She put her arms around him and smooching him on the cheek, or was it the neck, Ophelia couldn't quite see. It better not have been the neck she thought. No wonder he keeps coming around, given all of the attention and food he gets. Then she remembered he was only there because she invited him. Repeatedly. Still, he seemed to be enjoying Stella's company too much.

Ophelia walked Trey out to his car. She gave him a hug before he climbed in. It was then that she noticed a white van driving down the road. It looked like the van she had seen previously. Perhaps it was connected to a local business, but still it triggered a bad feeling. It was pointless to ask Trey to follow it. It would be long gone by the time he got through the gate onto the road, and anyway, she couldn't send him off chasing her wild suspicions. He would ask too many questions, especially relating to Stella, that she just wasn't at liberty to answer.

Ophelia and Stella settled in for the evening. It was another breathless frosty night, with an eerie mist that hung at about shoulder height. It was rather bizarre, especially with a partial moon that created an eerie glow. There were the usual noises coming from outside, which the women were starting to get used to.

Ophelia was in her study watching a movie on the computer. She had headphones on so she wouldn't disturb Stella and could blank out distractions. The lights were dimmed as Stella sat in one of the large chairs in the lounge room. From time to time, when there was an unusual noise, she would push the curtain aside and peep out the window.

There was the sound of breaking glass and then Stella screaming. It was loud enough to he heard clearly through the headphones. Immediately, Ophelia jumped up and rushed into the lounge room. Stella was crouched down in the corner and there was glass on the floor.

"What happened?" she asked.

"I don't know," Stella said. "I just took a peep out the window and then it shattered, so I jumped out of the way."

For some reason, Ophelia looked at the wall opposite the window and there was a chunk missing from the plaster. She went over to look closer and could see something metallic on the floor directly beneath it. She bent down to pick it up and immediately recognized it as a bullet. She turned to Stella with a look of dread and said, "Stay down, someone is shooting at you."

While bent over, she quickly went around and turned off the inside lights. As she got to the switch near the front door, she turned on the porch light and picked up her axe handle. Then, while fumbling in the dark, they made their way up the stairs and into her bedroom. There was a small fire burning and this gave them some light.

She whispered to Stella, "Quick, give me your phone."

Stella felt her pockets and then replied, "I don't have it. I think I dropped it on the floor next to the window when I jumped up."

"Damn!" Ophelia said. "Mine is in the study and out of charge. I was going to plug it in when I went to bed. Shit!"

"Then we should go down and get mine, yes?" Stella said.

"I don't know. I suppose we could get both and then I can charge mine."

"Ok, then we both go now," Stella said.

Now that their eyes had adjusted to the dark, the small amount of light that entered the house from the front and back porch lights allowed them to just make out the stairs. They began to descend when the outside lights went out.

"They've turned off the power," she whispered. The only light now was the pittance that bled into the hallway from the fire in her bedroom. She descended another step, Stella holding on close behind her, when they heard the smashing of glass. It was the sound that is made when someone is clearing away broken glass so they can get their arm in to access the latch. Immediately she pushed back against Stella, almost knocking her over. Then, clumsily, they both stumbled back up the stairs into Ophelia's room and quietly closed the door. There was no lock on the door, so she carefully propped a chair against the handle. It may hold off a determined intruder for ten or twenty seconds if they were lucky.

"What will we do, can we hide?" Stella asked as she looked around the room. There was a wardrobe, but it would be the first place an intruder would look.

"No, we have to get out. But first we need to dress for the cold," Ophelia said as she thew a jacket and jeans onto the bed and then rummaged around for socks and sneakers.

"Quick put these on or you will freeze," Ophelia

said to Stella, as she put on her own jacket and boots.

She pushed her hand through the closed curtains and quietly opened the door to the balcony. Then when they had both gone through, she locked it behind her. That may give them another twenty seconds. Every obstacle she could put between themselves and their pursuers, was one step closer to safety. They would now have to climb over the iron railing and lower themselves down to the rear porch.

She grabbed the iron; it was wet and bitterly cold. By morning it would be covered in ice. Neither of them was wearing gloves, but they would have to lower themselves down by holding the iron bars and hope that their feet could touch the porch below. Once they were on the roof of the porch, they would have to somehow slide down the corner poles that held it up. This was going to be difficult seeming the porch roof and gutter overhung those poles. But presently, there was no better plan.

Ophelia went down first, slowly lowing herself as her feet dangled in mid-air. It was dark below and she couldn't see the porch roof, she just knew it was there somewhere. She reached full stretch and still there was no porch. It could have been just millimeters away, it may have been a meter away, or she may have forgotten its exact location and was about to miss it completely.

"Hurry," Stella whispered. "There is a flashlight

coming from one of the upstairs windows."

There was nothing for it but for Ophelia to let go and trust her memory. She took a breath and then let go. She must have only been millimeters away because she barely felt any fall. She whispered,

"I'm on the porch roof, hurry down."

Stella quickly followed her. Ophelia grabbed her legs so that she knew she was there to catch her.

They pressed themselves against the cottage wall just as the balcony door rattled, and a flashlight shone through the glass lighting up the mist beyond. They couldn't be seen in their current position, however, if their pursuers came into the back yard and shone their torches back at the house, then they would be fully exposed. Fortunately, by the light of the torch they could just make out how far it was to the ground.

When the flashlight disappeared, Ophelia said, "I think we should hang off the roof and then jump the rest of the way. I'm just worried we may make a noise when we land. What do you think?"

"We jump," Stella said without a moment's hesitation.

So, as before, they lowered themselves down as far as possible and then let go. Each of them made a soft thud when they landed, and as they sprang to their feet Ophelia said, "Follow me."

Due to repeated trips, she knew exactly where the woodshed was, despite being invisible. She counted her steps; it should be about forty-five.

With Stella holding on to her jacket, Ophelia took the lead into the void. She figured that by the time they reached the woodshed they would be safe from the flashlight beams as they were dissipated by the mist.

With her hands out in front she groped until she touched the leaves of a small tree. That must be the tree that grew to the left of the woodshed. This meant she was a couple of meters to the side of it. This was good. She could get her bearings from here. She felt for the trunk of the tree and then crouched down pulling Stella with her.

"What do we do now?" Stella asked. "We can't stay here like this; we will freeze by morning. And what if they are still here at morning? We must have a plan."

Ophelia thought about it and then said, "If we can go to the shed, and get inside one of the vehicles, then maybe we could drive away." She felt in her pockets, damn, the keys were in the house. The pickup's keys were the easiest to get to, they were on a small table just inside the front door.

She whispered to Stella, "This is the plan. We will make our way to the shed by taking a broad arc through the vineyard-side paddock. Then you will hide in the shed on the left-hand side of the pickup. I will creep up to the front door and hopefully slip my hand around the frame and grab the keys. Then I will sneak back to the shed, we get in, I start the pickup and we take off before they can stop us."

"And what if they have the driveway blocked, like up at the gate? It is what I would do," Stella said in an all too knowing and creepy way.

"Good point," Ophelia said. "Then we shall head to the back gate and escape through the dairy paddocks. If someone is at the dairy, then we can raise the alarm by calling the police."

Ophelia sensed that Stella was uncomfortable with her mentioning the police. She couldn't see her in the dark, but it was her silence that suggested she wasn't in agreement.

CHAPTER 13

The women made what they believed was a broad arc that should bring them to the far side of the shed where the vehicles were kept. On several occasions they stepped in what they believed to be cow poo. There was nothing they could do about it but just grimace and bare it. It was probably the first time that Stella had suffered such things; at least she was wearing Ophelia's sneakers.

As they got closer to the shed there were obstacles on the ground, such as old timbers and abandoned building stones. This slowed them down and forced them to grope and stumble, sometimes on all fours. It was dangerous and the risk of a sprained ankle or a serious fall was real. Finally, Ophelia found the wall and followed it along to the entrance. By this time, they were seeing flashlights in the back yard. There were at least two intruders, possibly more. One had walked down as far as the woodshed, so they were lucky they didn't stay there, and now they were heading back, or so the beams of light suggested.

Stella went inside the shed, feeling her way along the side of the pickup truck, and whispered to

Ophelia, "You go, while they are still out the back."

Using her spatial recollection, and with as much speed as she dared, she made it to the corner of the house and then felt her way along the front wall. At times she stumbled over things that she had planted in a small flower garden and forgotten about, until finally she was at the step leading to the porch.

She carefully climbed up while feeling for the door. Would it be open or closed? Then, as she thought she was about to touch the door, the porch light came on, bright and blinding. One of the intruders must have turned the main power back on. The breaker box was on the far wall of the house, so now she knew that one intruder was there, and the other was in the back yard. Were there more? Would there be someone just inside the doorway? Would they grab her hand as she reached for the keys?

After her eyes adjusted, she could see the door was ajar. She pushed against it, and it silently opened. The cottage was dark inside with only the light from the porch streaming into the lounge. She quickly poked her head around the entrance, expecting the keys to be sitting on the table. Yes, there they were. She reached out and grabbed for them. Then like a cat, she sprung down off the step and headed as fast as she could back to the shed where Stella was waiting. It was easier now that there was some light, but that also raised the risk of being spotted. There were now flashlight beams on both sides of the house. One from the person who had turned the power back on, and the other from the person coming up from the back yard. She had to move quickly, or they were going to get caught in a pincer movement.

She bolted into the shed she said, "Stella, get to the passenger door and be ready to jump in as soon as I unlock it."

"OK, I am ready," Stella said as she placed her hand on the door handle.

Here was the problem. As soon as Ophelia used the remote to unlock the pickup, there would be a beep and the indicators would flash. The light and sound would be unmistakable, alerting their pursuers and bringing them straight down on them. She would have to get them both into the vehicle, get it started, reverse out of the shed and then drive around to the back gate, all without being shot, or having the vehicle disabled by getting riddled with bullets.

However, the flashlight beams were getting closer, and she could not hesitate any longer. It was like starting a fire walk. Once that first step was taken, they couldn't stop, they couldn't turn back. Forward was the only option. Thinking it may be quieter than using the remote button on the key fob, she flicked out the key, and after feeling about, inserted it into the door lock. She was right. When she turned it there was no beep or flashing of lights. However, as soon as they opened the doors, the interior light came on. She climbed up into the driver's seat, and reaching over quickly, turned it off. Given that their eyes were so accustomed to the dark, the interior light seemed really bright. Would it have been so bright that their pursuers would have seen it?

With that possibility she had no choice but to put the key straight into the ignition and turn it on. The motor roared to life, and she immediately slammed it into reverse and floored the accelerator. She did it so quickly that it was only after they were reversing that they managed to close the doors.

Ophelia said, "Get down as low as you can. Maybe they won't chase us if they think it is only me in the truck."

Stella slid down in her seat, although she could still see just over the dash and the bottom of the passenger window.

When clear of the shed, Ophelia slammed the brakes on, put it into forward and again planted the accelerator to the floor. The engine roared and all four wheels spun. Up to this point she hadn't turned on the lights, instead planning to be like a phantom in the mist. A vehicle that they wouldn't see coming until she was right on top of them. She knew the layout of the front paddock and the size of the yard, so hopefully she could avoid obstacles while keeping the porchlight's diffused glow on her lefthand side.

Stella yelled out, "There is a man, hit him, hit him."

In the high-speed confusion Ophelia just aimed for him. It looked like he was reaching for something in his jacket. She figured it was probably a gun. Despite swerving, and getting extremely close, the vehicle was going to miss him, and they would drive right on past. Then as at the very last second Stella thrust her door open, somehow pushing it out with her leg. There was a thud as they hit the man, and immediately Stella yelled, "Stop, stop!"

Like before, she yelled so aggressively that Ophelia just slammed on the brakes without thinking. Stella flew forward and hit the dash, but she was not injured. She quickly jumped out and ran back to the man lying on the ground, and then just a quickly back to the pickup truck shouting,

"Go, Go, Go! He is OK, it was not serious." There was some blood on Stella's hands, that she casually wiped on her pants.

Upon noticing Ophelia said, "Oh my God, are you hurt?"

Stella casually said, "It is not mine, do not worry about it."

Ophelia found it rather confusing. The man was trying to kill her, she wanted to run him over, and then hits him with the car door. Why would she then want to stop to check if he was alright? Maybe she knew him, maybe it was her former husband.?

It was just such a strange thing to do given their situation.

Stella put on her seatbelt as Ophelia took off with a roar across the paddock. There was a loud smashing sound that came from behind them, and then a series of thuds. Ophelia looked back and saw that a bullet had come through one of the rear windows. They were lucky it hadn't smashed the window, but instead there was a small hole surrounded by spider cracks. God knows where the bullet had exited, probably out through the trim and panel of the opposite door. She figured that the other thuds were bullets hitting the pickup truck's body. She hoped that no serious damage had been done, like hitting the fuel tank, or a tire that was now deflating as they drove.

When she thought she had gained sufficient distance, and immersion into the mist, she turned on the headlights. It was pointless using the powerful spotlights, they would just reflect back at her in the thick fog and make it even harder to see. So, she jumped and bumped the vehicle through the paddock at high speed on low beam. There, in front she could see the gate. She had to slam on the brakes and attempt to swing the back of the truck around as if she was drifting. Then when it was lined up, she roared through the gate and off across the dairy paddock.

A black cow emerged from the mist directly in front of them and she had to swerve hard to miss it. They were lucky that they didn't roll the truck. Expecting more cows ahead, she slowed down to half the previous speed. She knew the gates would be open all that way to the dairy buildings, and only there would they have to stop to open the gate that would let them onto the dairy tracks.

However, as they approached the final gate the vehicle slowed right down. The ground had become very boggy from all of the wash water from the dairy and being churned into mud by the cows. The vehicle was in 4WD and snaked wildly as they made slow progress toward the gate. It would have been a terrible place to get bogged and would put a dismal end to their escape bid.

Finally, they reach a concrete ramp that took them out of the mud. She stopped, got out, and ran over to the gate, opened it, and drove through, then stopped to close it again.

Stella was amazed that Ophelia would do this and she yelled, "What the hell are you doing?"

"I had to close it," she said. "They have been so good to me and if I didn't then all of the cows might get out," Ophelia said as she climbed back up into the vehicle.

"Oh my God!" Stella said. "You are such a wannabe angel."

Ophelia wasn't sure if that was a complement or an insult, but under the circumstances it didn't warrant any further thought.

From where they were parked Ophelia could see

the road that ran across the front of her property. Through the fog she could also see that headlights from at least two vehicles had turned on and were now heading toward the dairy via the main road. Her original plan was to wake up Reggie, assuming that he was actually on sight, and then try to get assistance either from him or the police. But now that seemed like a bad plan. If she did not get off the dairy property and onto the main road, then she would be trapped in here, with the only option being to get back out into the paddocks and try to find another way to escape.

It had not occurred to her that she should have driven straight through the wire fences. Sure, there would have been damage to the vehicle, and of course the fences would be wrecked, and the cows would get out. Still, given the stress that she was under, she'd done exceptionally well to get them as far as she had. Thus, the oversight was understandable and forgivable.

There were some security lights illuminated around the dairy, and even down the paved drive that led to the main road. She turned off her main lights and relied on the parking lights. She also avoided using the brakes as much as she could. Instead, she would use emergency the handbrake in order to stop the brake lights from illuminating and giving away their position.

Thus, stealthily she made it to the main road, and then rapidly took a series of side roads, as they appeared, hoping to escape detection and put distance between themselves and the pursuers. Finally, Ophelia turned up a secluded holler and turned the truck off.

She faced Stella and demanded, "Who the hell were those people and why are they after you?"

Stella let out a long sigh, "They are sicario. They work for my husband; I mean my former husband."

"They are what?" Ophelia asked.

"Sicario, you maybe call them hitmen, or assassins. They are professional."

"We need to get to the police," Ophelia said.

"No, we cannot. They will expect this and be waiting for us. This is a small country place, there may only be one or two policemen on duty. They will wait outside the police station for us. We cannot do this, not tonight. They probably know that we do not have the telephone, so we cannot call for any help."

"Why does your former husband want you dead?" Ophelia asked.

"It is complicated, but in short it is because I know too much. I can connect him and his business partners to many crimes that will put them in prison, both here in Australia, and also in other countries. This is also why my children are away. They are hiding in other countries so he cannot use them to force me."

Then Ophelia asked, "So why aren't the police protecting you. Isn't there some witness protection program or something?" she asked.

"Yes, there is, and I was using it but then it got compromised. So, until they work out how he has infiltrated it, I needed somewhere to stay. But his organization is very well connected, and it seems that it was compromised again. This I am very surprised about, for you are a nobody who lives in a nowhere place."

Ophelia knew what she meant, even if it had come across as quite insulting.

Then she said, "You don't suppose he is tracking your phone, or maybe has a tracker in your bag or on your clothes? Today's technology is frightening like that. It seems the government and military can find anyone anywhere as soon as they log into something."

"This is possible," Stella said. "I have used my cell phone, although it was new with a new number, but still maybe it is being tracked. And to be honest, I have not gone through every bit of luggage and clothing. Maybe it is me who is the leak and I just don't know it."

Ophelia said, "Well maybe we have given them the slip this time. We don't have phones or luggage with us, and you are mainly wearing my clothes. So provided we stay off the main roads, and keep out of sight, then we may escape them. At least for now."

Ophelia had a flashlight in the pickup. In fact, it

was already in it when she bought it. Apparently, the former owner though it a good idea to have one that continually charged from the vehicle. She grabbed it then got out and walked around to inspect the damage.

On the lefthand side they had copped a spray of bullets, fortunately missing the wheels and fuel tank. The last bullet in the line was the one that went through the rear window. It had exited though the roof on the opposite side, about thirty centimeters behind Ophelia's head. She had been extremely lucky. Indeed, they had both been extremely lucky.

She got back into the car, and they sat there in dark silence. Already the windows were fogging up, and given where they were parked, they would have no warning if the hitmen were closing in on them.

Finally, Ophelia said, "We can't stay here. They know we wouldn't have gone too far, so if they just take all of the side roads, they will eventually discover us."

"I agree," Stella said. "But where to go? We must hide somewhere away from the road, and preferably where it is warm."

Ophelia turned on the satellite navigation. The road they were on showed up, as well as their position. She was surprised how far they had travelled from the cottage, as they headed further from town, paved roads, and farms, and out into the wilderness. Indeed, they were at the edge of a

National Park. It was likely if they continued on this track that they would get blocked by locked gates or be forced to negotiate rough and perilous fire tracks. Not best done at night, and especially in thick fog. Furthermore, the trip from her cottage to the dairy was the first real four wheel driving she had ever done, so she was just winging it and learning as she went.

She typed 'Lifecycle Retreat' into the navigation. There was an insignificant track that led from the road they were currently on, through some rugged terrain, and then onto the lodge property. However, the navigation said they couldn't get through, even though the track was definitely there. Maybe it was because of locked gates or crossing through private property. Still, they decided to give it a go. She was betting that the hitmen didn't have offroad vehicles, hence, they wouldn't be able to follow them on their chosen route.

The question that remained, however, is would they anticipate that she would try to reach Trey? They had probably seen him at the cottage while it was under surveillance. But had they connected him to the lodge? Would she be putting him in danger by going there? She didn't know, but she was confident Trey would know what to do if they could only get to him.

CHAPTER 14

It was only 9 o'clock in the evening. It had only been two hours since the first shot was fired, and yet so much had happened that if felt like hours. If she could get straight through to the lodge, then hopefully Trey would still be awake.

She said to Stella, "We'll continue down this road," and then as she pointed to the navigation she said, "then we'll turn off here and cut across to the lodge property where Trey is. We should be able to get some help and shelter there."

"This is a good plan," Stella said. "They will be watching the main road that goes in," and she pointed to a part of the map, "but they will not see the track that comes in from the bottom, this one, our track."

Ophelia kept the main lights off, and instead crawled down the road using only the parking lights. The navigation map would alert them when they needed to turn onto the first sidetrack. Five minutes later they saw it in front of them just where it was supposed to be. It didn't look like much, and probably would have been impassable after a heavy shower of rain. Fortunately, it hadn't rained for weeks, it was just the heavy dew that settled every night that kept the landscape damp and green.

They bumped down the remote track, as leaves and branches scraped along the side of the truck, and the wheels bounced across rocks and gullies. Soon though it was getting too difficult and dangerous to continue without the headlights. Ophelia decided to turn them on hoping they would be well out of site from the hitmen. In the full light they could see how perilous their journey was and would be. There was a steep gully on one side of the track. They could not see down to the bottom, but at times their wheels must have been just centimeters from disaster.

Up ahead was a steep climb so she put the vehicle into low four-wheel drive and engaged all the diff locks, just like Trey had shown her when they took it for a test drive.

Without taking her eyes off the road, and holding onto the handle above the passenger door, Stella said, "You've got this. Just slow and steady and we get there."

The vehicle crawled up the hill, every now and then the wheels would slip, rocks would be dislodged, and then it would grip again. Further along the track they came across a downed tree that was blocking their way. She remembered how Trey had shown her how to operate the winch.

They both jumped out, and as Ophelia operated

the winch controls, Stella walked the cable out until it reached the downed tree. Had the diameter and weight been any greater they would have been stuck. Fortunately, it was small enough to hook the cable around and winch it at an angle until there was enough room for them to slip the vehicle past.

It took them nearly an hour to get to the boundary fence between the National Park and the lodge property.

Damn, there was a gate, and it was locked. Probably Trey had a key, but that did them no good at the moment.

"What now?" Stella said.

"Maybe we can push it over," Ophelia suggested.

"Yes, do this. It is not big," and then sarcastically added, "And there are no cows."

Ophelia reversed back and then lined up the hitching post. It didn't look like it was very strong. It was more a symbolic fence rather than one designed for security, or for stopping large animals like cattle and horses. She slowly edged the truck up until it touched the post, and then crept forward. The post pushed over with little effort until the gate popped and swung free. They were through and maybe had another ten minutes of rough bush track until they arrived at the lodge complex.

When they arrived at the first cabin there were lights illuminating paths that connected the guest accommodation and other outbuildings. It was a relief to see evidence of civilization. Ophelia parked the truck behind one of the buildings to conceal it, and then they proceeded on foot. She had never been this far into the lodge, and all they could do to find their way was to follow the paths and signs back up the hill face upon which it sprawled.

Eventually, they arrived at the reception building, but it was locked, and the lights were turned off. Using her flashlight, she looked around to see if there was any intercom or night button that could get her through to Trey. She had no idea where he lived, or indeed, even if he was on site at this time. She found the button, pushed it, and then waited. After a couple of attempts a voice answered. It was a woman's voice and she sounded like she had just been woken up.

"Hello, Lifecycle Retreat, how can I help you?"

Damn, it was Francesca. She was afraid that she may answer.

"Hello, this is Ophelia. May I please speak to Trey, it is urgent," she said.

"I'm sorry who is this?" Francesca asked.

"It is Ophelia, from Lavender Cottage. We have met. I deliver dairy and baked goods to the Retreat. I need to speak to Trey, please."

"I'm sorry but Trey is not available," Francesca said in an annoyed tone. "If it is not something that I can help you with, then you will have to come back tomorrow morning. He will be available after 7.30am."

"No, you don't understand, it is really

important. Can you please just tell me what cabin he is in so I can discuss this with him directly?" Ophelia said with increasing desperation.

"I'm sorry, I can't do that. That is private, and I'm sure there is no cake or scone emergency that you can't either discuss with me, or that cannot wait until morning," she said in an angry condescending voice.

"I can't explain it to you, but it is very important that I talk to him now," Ophelia insisted.

"I'm sorry, but you sound like you are drunk or on drugs. If you do not leave, then I will have to call the police," she said in a cold voice.

Stella put her hand over the intercom button and then said to Ophelia, "No police. They will lead the sicario straight to us. They will be expecting us to contact the police, in fact they are probably counting on it."

Ophelia pushed the button one last time and said, "No need to call the police. We will take the issue up with Trey in the morning. Sorry to have bothered you."

Francesca replied, "Please leave the property," and then went silent.

"What to do now?" Sella asked.

"We will just have to find him. We can start by looking for his pickup truck. I can only assume that he would have parked out front of where he is living."

They walked over to a site map on a notice

board and read it by flashlight. There were clusters of cabins spread over a wide area. Most were designated by numbers and names. Then there were a few that either had no designation, or they were marked as private. On one of them it said, 'Caretakers Residence'.

"Do you think it is this one?" Stella said as she pointed to it.

"I don't know, but it's probably a good place to start. However, the last thing we want to do is knock on Francesca's door," she said.

God she was hoping that Trey was not sharing accommodation with Francesca, or even worse, that they were sharing a bed. No, surely not. He'd given no indication that anything like that was happening. But then again, tonight had already been filled with surprises and the unimaginable, so who knew? Her world was already turned upside down, what difference would one more rotation make.

Quietly, they weaved along the paths and boardwalks. Now that they were out of their vehicle, they were getting very cold. When they escaped the cottage, the adrenaline had kept them warm, and then in the pickup they had the heater blasting them with hot air. But now that they were outside, and the pace had slowed, they were really feeling the cold. The lodge was also on the exposed side of a plateau and there was a breeze that added significantly to the windchill.

There was a carport, and something was parked inside. Ophelia had been vary sparing in using the flashlight just in case Francesca was watching from a window somewhere, but she turned it on to reveal Trey's pickup truck. Excellent, she thought.

The problem now was that they were faced with a double cabin that had two doors side by side. Perhaps Trey lived on one side and Francesca on the other. Which door would be his? And furthermore, if she knocked on one door, how could she stop the other cabin from hearing the sound. They knew that Francesca had been woken up, and may still be awake, but Trey may be deep asleep and not hear the knocking.

They were out in the country, in at a relatively isolated location, so maybe Trey didn't even lock his door. Or, if he locked his front door, then maybe he didn't lock the back door, or perhaps not lock the windows. Perhaps she should try all of them first.

When they arrived at the side-by-side doors. Stella whispered, "Look," as she pointed to some work boots at the entrance to one of the cabins.

Although Ophelia did not recognize them, it was assumed they must be Trey's. They certainly wouldn't have belonged to Francesca. But what if they were another employee, like a maintenance man or something? What if she broke into the cabin and it was a stranger? How would she explain that, and what kind of trouble might she get into?

She tried the front door, and it was locked. Then

she whispered to Stella, "You stay here. I'm going to try around the back to see if it is also locked." Stella nodded silently.

As quietly as she could Ophelia crept around to the back. She thought to herself, 'I hope they don't have a dog'. Trey hadn't mentioned one, but still maybe whoever was in the other cabin may have one. That was the last thing she wanted, to come across a guard dog that barked and woke everyone up, or even worse, attacked her. Fortunately, there was no fencing at the rear, so it was likely that if there were any dogs, they would be inside the cabin. Oh, that didn't sound good either. Best not to think about it.

She tried the back door and it opened. As she pushed, it creaked. It was completely dark inside and she had no option but to turn on the flashlight before taking another step.

The cabin was warm, and it smelt like it was inhabited by a man rather than a woman. She passed through the laundry and saw a man's clothes. Then as she looked into the bathroom, she did not see cosmetics that would indicate it was being used by a woman. Now she was in the living room, it was neat and basic, looking like a typical hotel room. Off to the side was what she imagined was the bedroom. It must have been a single bedroom cabin. Well, that was a good sign. She walked over to the front door and quietly unlocked and opened it.

Putting her finger up to her lips she gestured to Stella to be quiet and beckoned her to come in. Ophelia thought it best that Stella come into the warmth, and that whatever they were about to face, they faced it together.

How were they going to approach this next challenge? She looked around the living room to see if there were any signs that it was in fact where Trey was staying. Perhaps an envelope with his name on it, or a bill or notice stuck to the door of the refrigerator. There had to be something somewhere.

She flashed the light about and saw some papers in the corner of the kitchen. She crept over and picked one up. It was addressed to Mr. T. Maccabee, bingo, this must be it. She looked at another and it said Trey, and then another and it said Francesca and Trey Maccabee. What the hell she thought, and a cold shiver went down her spine. Did that mean they were married, or maybe Francesca was his sister. No, she couldn't be his sister; they didn't look anything alike. Anyway, he would have mentioned if she was his sister. Maybe it was just a typing error, or the way it had been written that gave a wrong impression.

Regardless, their current situation was more serious than her silly fears, and desires. Who cared what was happening between Trey and Francesca, if in fact anything at all? The pressing issue was that they were being hunted by hitmen and they needed some place safe to hole-up until the authorities could intervene.

She looked over and there was a phone on the wall. Perhaps she could use that? Didn't you normally dial 0 or 1 to get an outside line? No, that wouldn't do, it may go straight through to Francesca and then she would know they have broken into one of the cabins. Anyway, talking on the phone would probably wakeup whoever was behind the bedroom door. That is assuming there actually was someone in there. The cabin was warm so, yes, there must be someone here, and given all the evidence, it must be Trey.

There was no choice, she would have to open the bedroom door and shine the light inside to see if Trey was there in bed. It was both exiting and scary. Surely, he would be happy to see here. Stella crept in step behind Ophelia as she approached the door. Gently, she clasped the handle and began to turn it. Excellent, it wasn't locked, and she slowly pushed the door open. There was a slight creak, but not enough to wake someone. Light spilled into the room revealing a bed on the far side. There was someone in the bed, buried down under the doona with just a tussle of hair on the back of their head showing. Stella stayed in the doorway while Ophelia crept ever closer.

It certainly looked like Trey. It was about the right size body, as well as hair length and color. Unfortunately, she couldn't see his face. It was turned toward the wall and partly covered by a sheet. She looked around the room to see if she could recognize his clothes or anything else. On the chair there was a jacket. It looked very much like his, and there were also some tall cowboy boots. She thought she'd seen him wearing them at some point over the past week. Finally, she spied an acoustic guitar leaning up against the wall. Surely, this must be his room, everything she saw convinced her of that.

How should she wake him up? She started by softly calling his name, but he did not respond. She made sure not to shine the flashlight directly at him so he wouldn't be blinded if he rolled over and opened his eyes. Then she knelt down beside the bed and spoke his name again, this time putting her hand on his shoulder and gently shaking him. Finally, he seemed to wake up, rolling over and partially opening his eyes. It was strange that he was not startled, maybe he was still half asleep, like she was in his dream, a lucid dream. What a pleasant thought that was.

She kept saying, "Trey, wake up."

Then he opened his eyes fully and he said, "Ophelia, what are you doing here? What time is it? What, what... what are you doing here?"

She wasn't sure if he was still partly asleep, but he took hold of her hand that was on his shoulder and pulled it under the doona next to his cheek.

He held it there and said, "Your hand is so cold;

did you walk here?"

"Yes, well sort of," she said. "I'm here with Stella, we have a serious problem and need some help."

He responded in a groggy voice, "Anything babe."

CHAPTER 15

Trey got out of bed wearing his boxer shorts and nothing else. Ophelia could not help herself but watch as he put on jeans and a t-shirt. Of course she should have left the room, but she had told him not to turn on the light, and she did have the flashlight with her, so it was kind of an excuse. Stella remained in the doorway, no doubt also perving. After he got dressed, they went into the kitchen area and put on the kettle to make coffee.

He said, "OK, tell me everything, from the start."

Ophelia recounted the story.

"My former employer, the law firm, asked me to put Stella up for a week or so. She is testifying against her former husband and needed to be hidden away. There was a problem with witness protection, a leak, so they needed somewhere off-grid until they sorted out an alternative."

"So, who is she hiding from?" Trey asked.

Stella spoke up, "It is the Colombians and the Sicilians. Maybe the less you know the better, otherwise you also become a target."

Trey looked back at Ophelia and then asked Stella, "Is she a target?"

In a very calm and impassionate voice Stella said, "Probably. She has seen too much, and they do not know what I have told her. It would be good for them to get rid of her at the same time they do hit on me."

"Am I a target?" he asked in amazement.

"Probably not, but they may come looking for you when they are trying to find me. They have seen you at the cottage, they know you are Ophelia's boyfriend, so to find you would be good for them, yes?"

Ophelia looked at Trey, while he looked at her. 'Boyfriend'. He wasn't arguing or squirming, but still she felt embarrassed like a sixteen-year-old girl.

Then Ophelia continued, "Then tonight, at around 7pm, a shot got fired through the lounge window of the cottage."

"What!?" Trey exclaimed.

"It was intended for Stella but luckily it just missed her," Ophelia continued. "We escaped by climbing down the bedroom balcony, got into the pickup truck, and cut across the dairy land till we hit the bitumen road. Then we took the backtracks until we got to the bottom of your property. Oh, yeah, sorry, we busted your fence and gate."

"That's OK," he said.

"Right now, my pickup is parked next to the first cabin, the one that is farthest down the hill." she said.

"Have you called the police?" Trey asked.

"No, and we can't call the police, not yet anyway. If we call the police, then the hitmen may follow them straight to us. What I need to do is call my old law firm, the ones that arranged for Stella to stay with me. The problem is that neither Stella nor I have our cell phones. They are back at the cottage, and neither of us remember the number to call. That means I have to make a few calls, and hope those people answer, before I can get through to the right person."

Stella spoke, "I'm a bit worried that the sicario will come here looking. Is there somewhere we can go where they won't know to look?"

Trey thought for a while and then said, "I think I know the perfect spot. We have a secluded cabin on the far side of the property. It was one of the original settler buildings. It doesn't have power, and not much in the way of creature comforts, but no one will find us there. When we get there, you can use my phone to get in contact with your people."

He put on his warm clothes, and they gathered up extra blankets and pillows. He even got his beanie and put it on Ophelia's head, then a pair of gloves for her hands.

He said, "Here's something for those little cold hands of yours."

It was sweet and she felt comforted. And not to leave Stella out, he found a rustic knitted poncho to keep her warm.

They quietly made their way back down the paths until they reached Ophelia's pickup truck. She shone the flashlight on the bullet holes, and what seemed like a bad dream was once again real. Trey was shocked at how lucky they had been to escape. It was obvious that these gangsters meant business.

Ophelia suggested that Trey drive, given that he knew the way, and the condition of the track. She rode shotgun and Stella sat in the back seat.

The property was larger than Ophelia had imagined. It took them about twenty minutes to reach the cabin. It was on an exposed ridge affording a 360-degree view; not that they could see anything in the dark. It was shrouded in the blowing mist of low clouds. The breeze was considerably stronger than back at the main lodge complex, and the location felt extra cold and isolated.

It was a stone and wood structure that looked very old and run-down. When Trey saw the disappointment on their faces, he assured them that it was better on the inside than on the outside. There was a small outbuilding that was just large enough to hide the vehicle, and it even had barn-style doors that closed. By flashlight they walked over the granite bedrock, upon which the cabin was built, and went inside. Although they were out of the damp breeze, it was still biting cold inside.

Fortunately, there was a large pile of wood stacked up near a fire pit that dominated the center of the single room cabin. It was an interesting design for a settler building. It was more like something one would expect in Nordic mythology, with the central hearth and then a chimney that went up through the center of the room.

The women stood in silence while Trey busied himself starting a fire. Ophelia and Stella pulled down some bedding that was stacked in the corner and placed it around the fire pit. The ordeal had taken more out of Stella than she had been letting on. Within a very short time, she lay down on a straw-packed hessian mattress with a pillow under her head and a blanket over her body, and just crashed. One minute she was awake, and the next she was completely out of it.

The fire illuminated the cabin, and as it grew, Trey went from window to window making sure that no light could escape and give away their position. They had running water, piped in from a rainwater tank, but it was only cold. All hot water had to be boiled on the fire. He rummaged through the kitchen cupboards and found a kettle, tin mugs, tea bags, long-life milk, and sugar.

He held the mugs up and asked, "Do you feel like a cuppa?"

"Ooh, yes please," Ophelia replied, as she settled down in front of the fire.

The kettle had to go directly onto the fire, and

compared to her woodstove, it took a long time to boil.

While they were waiting Trey found a packet of biscuits. He explained that the cabin was used as a refuge for hikers in bad weather and for overnighting. He visited the cabin regularly to ensure it was stocked with basic supplies. The cabin was part of a trail network that went for several hundred kilometers along the mountain range. There was probably someone passing through every couple of days in the summer months, but less so in the winter.

As he was pouring the hot water there was a strong gust of wind that howled and caused the cabin to creak.

"There is a change coming through," he said. "I saw it on the weather channel earlier this evening. We may even get a storm and some rain. In fact, it sometimes snows up here. It doesn't hang around on the ground for very long, but it looks really pretty when it does."

"Well, it certainly feels cold enough," she said.

After giving her the cup of tea he then handed her his cell phone.

"Thank you, I better start ringing the numbers I can remember, and then hope that they answer at this time of the night," she said.

She called several numbers but none of them answered, so she left voice and text messages, and then put the phone down next to her.

"Hopefully, someone will call or text me back," she said. "I never realized how lost I would be without my phone."

"Same here," Trey said.

Rain started to fall on the cabin's tin roof, and the gusts of wind became stronger.

"I think we're going to get a storm." And as he said that there was a loud rumble of thunder.

It made her shudder, and she pulled the blanket tighter about her shoulders.

Trey said, "It sounds like Captain Thunderbolt is going to pay us a visit."

"I've never heard that expression before," she said while giving him a look of confusion.

"You know, Captain Thunderbolt? The legendary gentlemen bush ranger?" he said.

She just stared blankly and shook her head indicating she had no idea what he was talking about.

"OK, let me explain," he said. "A bushranger used to haunt these mountains. Well, he was based a couple of hundred kilometers South of here, but he probably rode past this very spot and may have even stopped and taken shelter in this cabin. His real name was Frederick Ward, but he took on the name Captain Thunderbolt, and he would hold up travelers and stagecoaches on the main road between here and Uralla, in New South Wales. Apparently, his wife was also a bushranger and worked alongside of him."

"So, what happened to him?" she asked.

"Apparently, in 1870 he was hunted down after a robbery, cornered and shot dead," he said.

"So, it's not just a legend it's all true?" she asked.

"Yes, definitely, it's all in the public record. And further South there is a road called 'Thunderbolt's Way' that runs from Gloucester to Inverell."

"And what about the thunder, is that just tall tales and superstition, or do people actually see his ghost on stormy nights," she asked with wide eyes.

"I can't really say," Trey said. "Personally, I haven't seen anything. But we do get wicked thunderstorms here, especially in the springtime. There are lots of people that hike or trail ride through these mountains. Maybe the combination of storms, people camping in the wilderness, and tall tales of bushrangers and their ghosts... Well, you know what people's imaginations are like."

So there Trey sat. His feet against the stones at the base of the fire pit, legs stretched out, and his back and head propped up by pillows that rested against an old chair. Stella had said 'he was there for the taking'. It probably didn't get any more perfect 'for the taking' than their current setting. Yet, Ophelia was not like Stella. She was not someone who could pick whatever fruit she fancied. She had always waited for the fruit to drop into her lap, as to put it. Yet, God damn, he wasn't making any moves on her. Instead, he was being the perfect gentleman, and that wasn't really what she wanted.

Not now, and especially after what Stella had said, and the intentions that Stella may harbor.

There was only one solution. She lay herself down with her head in his lap and pulled the blanket up to her face. He put his hand down on her head and stroked her hair. It was funny that he just kept on talking as if it was a completely natural thing for her to do, as if they had been together for a whole lifetime, or many lifetimes. As if they were ancient soul mates.

The storm intensified but the cabin was solid. It had endured many such storms for over one hundred and seventy years. And even though it creaked and rattled, and each thunderous boom shook everything down to the floor, the tempest was kept at bay. It was as if they were living in the time of Thunderbolt, dry and warm in their own hideout. She was beginning to doze off and Trey had fallen silent as he stared into the flames. His legs must have started to go numb, and he gently lifted her head and pulled them out from underneath her.

She instantly got a feeling of disappointment and rejection. He was rejecting her advance, as subtle and timid as it was. It was as much courage as she could muster, and still he was pulling away. Then as she was about to pout and sulk, he lay down behind her and put his arms around so she could rest on one of his arms and be cradled by the other. 'Spooning'. That's what they call it, she thought to herself. She pushed back into him and fell asleep.

CHAPTER 16

When Ophelia woke up, she was alone by the fire. It took her a moment to get her bearings. Why was she here? That's right, last night, Stella getting shot at, escaping, and Trey, where was Trey? She sat up and looked around. It was only a one room cabin, and she was the only one inside of it. She got up and let the blanket fall to the mattress. Trey must have stoked the fire while she slept because the room was toasty warm. The windows were still covered so she went to the door and opened it.

Outside she found Stella and Trey sitting on a log seat, each with a mug of hot coffee. Both of them had blankets wrapped around them as they looked out over the valley beyond. It had snowed in the early hours of the morning and there was a blanket of white beneath a brilliant blue sky. It was an amazing and completely unexpected scene. Since living in the high country, she had seen frost on most mornings, but snow looked very different. It was brighter and formed a more complete blanket.

She walked over and sat down beside him. He shifted closer and wrapped the blanket around both of them. He then handed her his phone and said that there were missed calls and messages for her. Oh, damn, she thought, I have to wake from this pleasant dream and get back to reality. She wrapped her arm around the inside of his and then started to scroll though the phone. 'Yes', Dee had called, so now she had her number and could call her back.

She called Dee and explained the situation, but she held off giving their exact location, just in case the leak was somewhere in Dee's office. The advice they were given was to stay put and someone would get back to them. Obviously, it was a very serious situation and various departments of police, and the Department of Justice had to be coordinated.

Trey then called up the kitchen at the lodge and asked them to prepare breakfast for them, as well as pack some additional supplies for a couple of days. Then he requested that they deliver everything using his pickup followed by a second vehicle so they could leave his pickup behind at the cabin. He gave the excuse that he needed to get away and was staying out there with a friend. The less he told the staff the better.

Then he had to talk to Francesca. That would be challenging. Ophelia had explained what had happened last night, and how she had threatened to call the police. She also, finally, revealed how Francesca had been treating her over the previous weeks, as if she was a peasant or serf girl, and how she wouldn't even pass on her messages to Trey. He was genuinely shocked and said that he had never seen her behave like this before. Of course he hadn't, she hid it so well. Perhaps she saw Ophelia as a rival and a threat, so whatever she could do to sabotage any relationship between Trey and her would be done, covertly. Trey reserved until a later date, a full discussion with Francesca regarding Ophelia. For now, he just told Francesca that he was at the cabin with an old friend. He gave the impression it was an old buddy from his past.

About an hour after ordering their breakfast, it arrived. The two women hid behind a formation of giant granite boulders while the vehicles were unloaded. Trey told them that his friend had gone for a walk, trying to make it sound as inconspicuous as possible. The employees left his pickup, and then headed back down the track to the lodge. A marvelous hot breakfast had been prepared, perfect for the cold weather, and the additional supplies would keep them well fed for a few days.

Dee called back and said that a helicopter was being arranged to fly Stella out to a new location. It would be a police helicopter and that they would contact Ophelia directly to avoid their communications being compromised. They should expect it to arrive sometime around noon. It was also suggested that Ophelia should stay at the cabin for another day while the police did a sweep of the area, hoping to either catch the hitmen, or at least confirm that they were gone. The police would go to Lavender Cottage and collect Stella's belongings, and then maintain 24-hour surveillance for the next few days.

The helicopter called them up while it was enroute. As they waited outside, they could see it in the distance. The area around the cabin was clear and flat, so it had no difficulty in landing. Stella gave them both a hug and thanked them for everything they had done. She apologized for bringing so much trouble into Ophelia's life. However, she also suggested, privately, that without her, Ophelia may not have been as close to Trey. Also, while she was hugging Ophelia, she whispered something into her ear,

"When you are alone, look under the passenger seat of your car. Stay very quiet. You will understand."

It didn't make sense, but many things that Stella said didn't make sense until later. Stella also said she would post Ophelia's clothes back to her, and then climbed up into the helicopter. So much money and effort were being put into protecting Stella, it really must have been an important criminal case. The helicopter rose into the air and then shrank into the distance. And with that, all of the drama was gone. There they stood on the granite outcrop, looking out to the horizon with the cold wind blowing in their faces. She liked the way it tossed the long sandy curls that trickled from the bottom of his beanie.

What a situation to find themselves in. It was colonial, or even medieval. There they were on a barren windswept landscape, miles from anywhere, like Catherine and Heathcliff. They had a single room, no power, and no distractions. All they had was each other. Although it was how people had lived for most of human history, and pre-history, it was a completely unfamiliar experience for two children of the twentieth century, especially Ophelia. It was like finding oneself marooned with just one other person on a deserted island. Something one may read in a romance novel. It was all very well for her to put her arm around Trey when there were other people present. It was just being friendly and was constrained by modesty and social convention. But now it was just the two of them. It was raw and naked, every move meant something, anything could happen, thus the stakes were now so much higher.

They agreed they would stay at the cabin for one more night, and then return to the lodge for the following night, before going back to Lavender Cottage the day after that. Although the police had assured her that she would be safe, she tended to heed Stella's advice and erred on the side of caution. The sunsets from the cabin were amazing, as wisps of high cloud blazed orange in the West. It was going to be another clear cold night, so they collect wood and went inside to prepare dinner.

Trey was a surprisingly good cook. She wasn't sure why that surprised her, there was no reason why he shouldn't be. Perhaps, it was because he was accomplished in many other areas. How could someone be good at everything? Shouldn't he be good at some things and then bad at others? Perhaps with time his weaknesses would show. They ate a lovely stockman's meal despite half of it coming from packets and cans. It was a case of the simple things in life being the best. She would not have traded this meal for anything served in a Michelin Star restaurant, especially not the hot damper bread that they dipped into the minestrone medley that he had put together and boiled over the coals.

After eating they went outside to look up at the stars. The only light was a faint glow from the town over the Northern horizon. In front of them it was completely dark. Perhaps there were some farms out there on the distant hills, but they must have been sheltered from them, or the residents had already turned in for the night. The Southern sky was ablaze with the Milky Way in an enormous arc above them. They sat on the log seat with a blanket wrapped around them, counting meteors, and talking of esoteric and philosophical things.

After their cheeks got too cold, they went back

inside and lay in front of the fire, and although they still had Trey's phone, it remained untouched. They had a night that would remain a warm and comforting memory for the rest of their lives. Some parts of a story are best left to the imagination, and this was one of them.

They had cleaned and packed up the cabin by mid-morning and were ready to head back to the lodge. Just as they were about to leave a group of hikers arrived. It was good timing. The cabin was still warm and the kettle hot. The hikers had left a cabin further down the trail at dawn and were hoping to make the next cabin by nightfall. They shared a few stories, and Trey imparted some local knowledge and advice. Then he opened the out-building doors and Ophelia drove her pickup out into the daylight. The spray of bullet holes showed prominently down its side. The hikers were surprised at how such a thing could occur in Australia. They were from America and could understand it happening there, but here, with such strict gun laws, it seemed rather odd. Trey brushed it off as a hunting accident before the two of them drove off down the track.

They arrived back at the lodge and immediately locked Ophelia's pickup away in a shed.

He let her into one of the cabins and then said, "Wait here, I'll be back after I get everything organized. There will be clean towels and toiletries inside so you can have a shower. I'll see if I can get you some clean clothes from the gift ship. I'm guessing you are going to be a small adult. I'm sorry it might look a bit daggy, but it will do until we get you back home tomorrow."

With that he drove off and she was left alone for the first time since the whole ordeal began. The cabin was the same as the one he was living in. Neat and tidy, but generic and basic. Most guest activities at the lodge were conducted in communal areas, like the conference room, or out on the trails and 'gathering circles'. These 'circles' were firepits surrounded by large stones, erected in clearings around the property. The intention was to connect people with nature, and spirituality. They were like little Stone Henges, or similar. Trey was not so much into all these new-age rituals and philosophies, but he recognized that it was a huge market and so they catered to it.

The business she planned for Lavender Cottage would also tap into this. Not in a cynical way, but just to provide handmade, wholesome, healthy products, and experiences, for those that were searching for them. How others interpreted it was not Ophelia's concern; she was not on a mission to convert people. Trey had said that all the new-age stuff at the lodge was more Francesca's thing. Ophelia found this rather ironic given Francesca's unenlightened approach when dealing with people she deemed as below her, or from whom she could not winkle some money. Ophelia had decided Francesca was a fake hippie, regardless of whether she had all the facts or not.

She had a hot shower and then sat around in a robe, emblazoned with Lifecycle Retreat, and waited for Trey to return. There was a television in the living room, so she turned it on. It had been a long time since she watched television, and when she did, she found that the world had not changed. On the local news station there was no mention of hitmen, shootings, or desperate escapes. It was just politicians slagging politicians, and the obligatory good news story of some local kid done good in sport. What a waste of time, intelligence, and life. In the past she would have watched it, or scrolled on her phone, TikTok after stupid TikTok. But now her world had changed and become so much fuller and interesting.

One of the lodge employees arrived with clothes and lunch for her, although it was only a sandwich. Oh, how she already missed the fireside meals that Trey had cooked for her. The clothes included Lycra shorts she would have to use as undies, a t-shirt, and then sweatpants and a hoodie. All were boldly printed with the Lifecycle Retreat logo, but at least now she felt clean and comfortable, and if she stepped outside, she would blend in with the other guests.

Trey did not return until it was almost dark. He apologized profusely for leaving her alone for so long, explaining how there were many work-related things he needed to do. She said she completely understood, and apologized herself for dragging him away from his work for the past few days. He responded with a smile and said it was a welcome distraction. He then added that she made an excellent mascot for the lodge, as he laughed at her clothes.

He also said that he got an update from the police. Apparently, the white van she had seen on several occasions parked out front of her house, was found abandoned on the Gold Coast, 250km away. The authorities presumed the hitmen had slipped their net and fled the country.

What would Stella's advice be to her? Would she tell her not to trust the police and say that it was just a ploy to lure her out into the open again? If the mob could only know that she didn't know anything, then maybe they would leave her alone.

Well, perhaps there was one thing. She could identify the person she almost ran over out front of the cottage. Even though it was dark, she could still make out his face. And again, that same question? Why did Stella make her stop the pickup so she could go back to him as he lay on the ground? That also reminded her of what Stella had said about looking under the seat of the pickup. It was too cold, dark, and difficult now. She would have a look tomorrow.

They had dinner delivered. It was lovely, but

still paled compared to the romance of the previous night. Some things can never be duplicated.

Later in the evening Trey said, "I suppose I should get going, I've still got some things to do for work, and you must be tired."

She was a bit disappointed. Things were so comfortable. Why did he have to go, and how important were these things that he had to do? Was she rushing things? He had already spent the last two nights with her, and under circumstance that had been forced upon him, rather than of his own free will. Had she read this all wrong, was it just charity, or opportunity, on his part? She looked up at him but didn't say anything.

Then he said, "Do you want me to come back?"

She didn't say anything but just nodded her head.

He smiled and said, "Would it be OK if I brought some paperwork back with me?"

'Yay', so he really did have work to do. It wasn't just an excuse to get away. She smiled and nodded again. She didn't care if he did his taxes all night or rebuilt a lawnmower in the kitchen. She just didn't want to be alone. And not because she couldn't survive emotionally, or that she wasn't used to it. It's just that being with him was so much better, especially while she was away from her cottage home.

CHAPTER 17

Ophelia drove through her front gate. It was unlocked and open. The chain had been cut and left swinging loose for the past few days. It would have been done by either the hitmen or the police. She stopped, dragged it closed and then re-locked it. It was good to be home.

Down by the cottage she could see the wheel tracks left by the pickup as it had left ruts across the front paddock when Stella and she had made good their escape. She could even see where she had swerved and then braked after hitting one of the men.

At the front of the cottage one of the windowpanes was broken, but that was the only damage she could see. Inside, she could tell people had been throughout her home. Small things weren't quite in the right places. It bordered on the edge of recollection, but she could just a sense that others had been there. She immediately called a glazier, and they were able to send someone out that afternoon to repair the window. It would be too cold to leave it as it was, and anyway, she didn't like what it reminded her of. She also booked a visit from the local electrician. She wanted better outside lighting, including lights that illuminated the vehicle and firewood sheds.

The cottage was freezing cold, so she set to lighting both of the fires. It would take a day or two to get the building up to temperature again, so the earlier she started the better. She went into her study, and it was just as she had left it. The movie she had been watching just before the first shot was fired was paused, and the cell phone sat on her desk, blank and out of charge. The police must have collected Stella's phone, along with her clothes and other items, because despite looking, Ophelia could not find it.

She wondered where Stella was now, and what she was thinking. She was sure that Stella enjoyed staying at the cottage and valued the time that they spent together. Surely it would have been so much more interesting than a hotel room where she was probably holed up now. Maybe she had bodyguards she could talk to, or maybe they just sat silently outside the room, wearing suits and dark glasses like in the movies.

Ophelia recalled what Stella had whispered to her just before she was spirited away on the helicopter, "Check under the passenger seat". She went back outside to the truck and opened the passenger door. She put her hand underneath and felt around. Yes, there was something there, cold, and heavy. She pulled it out.

It was a handgun in brushed steel with a black grip. Down the side it read Beretta, Model 92FS 9MM Parabellum, made in Italy. Yeah, that figured. It looked just like the type of gun a sicario would use, or at least the 'Good Fellas' in the movies. So, this is what Stella did when she jumped out of the pickup and ran back to the man on the ground. She had grabbed his gun.

Ophelia put the gun down and felt around under the seat for anything else. When she pulled her hand out, she was holding two additional clips, each holding 10 rounds. That would mean, if the gun was fully loaded, then she would have 30 rounds of self-defense. There were bloody fingerprints smudged onto the additional clips. They would have been Stella's prints, but it wasn't her blood. It must have been from the man as she took the gun from him. However, Ophelia was surprised that there would have been blood. The most she could imagine from being hit with the door would have been a bloody nose.

She poked he head in and looked under the seat. There was something else back there and so she reached in further. It was hard to get to because it had slid and caught under the seat adjusting mechanism.

Eventually, her small hands were able to find their way in and dislodge it. She retrieved it to find that it was a small knife. One that had a concealed blade that shot out of the handle with the press of a button. She flicked it out and there was blood on it. She was not sure if it originally belonged to the hitman, or if it was something that Stella had carried upon her person. It was certainly small enough for Stella to conceal. Regardless, Ophelia surmised that when Stella had gone back to the man, she had either planned, or had taken the opportunity to stab him and then take his gun.

The police had made no mention of blood, or a body being found at the property. Ophelia could only assume that he was taken away by the hitmen. That may have been why they were able to escape; due to the hitmen being delayed as they attended to their wounded.

This was a surprising development. Ophelia had never fired a gun in her life, not even a paintball gun. Neither was she licensed to own or use a gun. She was sure that if she told anyone they would tell her to turn it over to the police. It probably had fingerprints on it that could identify the previous owner, and maybe it could be ballistically linked to other shootings, maybe even murders. Of course, now that she had put her hands all over it, then maybe they couldn't pull prints from it, she just didn't know.

She took the gun and knife inside, wiped the blood from the clips and the knife, and then put them gently on the desk in her study. She just stood there and looked at them for a while. She went into the kitchen, made a sandwich and hot chocolate, then came back into the study and just looked at them some more.

Yes, she would have to hand it all over to the police, it was the right thing to do, it was the law. But still, she was living through exceptional times. Perhaps she should hold onto it for tonight, and then call the police tomorrow and say she found all of it out in the paddock upon returning?

What if the police came now to check on her? They did say they were going to be watching the property and patrolling the roads. If they saw the gun, they would take it off her straight away. No, she didn't want that, so she opened the drawer and put everything inside. Then she thought to herself, if I ever had to use the gun, would thirty bullets be enough? She figured that she would be a pretty bad shot, so she may need to fire thirty bullets before even hitting anything. Her mind was racing, it was as if the gun had invaded her thoughts and made her think of things that she would never have considered before discovering it.

She felt both naughty and powerful at once. So, to suppress the intrusive thoughts, she locked it in the desk drawer, out of sight out of mind. Was she suffering from PTSD? The police had given her the phone number for a counsellor and said that she may need to call them if she was having difficulty dealing with the events of the past few days. Was harboring an illegal gun, and having fantasies of blowing away the bad guys, a sign of mental instability? She certainly would have thought so before she met Stella, but now she saw the world differently. She certainly had a heightened sense of fight or flight since the events of the other night. Was that, therefore, a response to trauma and was she becoming deluded? Or was this actually a rational and clear minded response to real and present danger? To her it all hinged on context.

She had to go into town, it was just going to be a quick trip to get some supplies. She would endeavor to remain as inconspicuous as possible. For this reason, she didn't take the shot-up truck, but instead her other car. She parked on the main street, and wearing a baseball cap and sunglasses, she popped into several shops. As she was returning to her car, she saw a sign that said, 'Guns and Ammunition'. She was drawn to it, and convinced herself that it wouldn't hurt to just have a quick look. It wasn't like she was going to get caught or reveal anything.

She pushed open the door. It was the first time she had even been in a shop like this, and she imagined it was perhaps what an adult sex shop or gambling den may have looked like. The door was reinforced with iron bars, and the windows with heavy mesh. Inside were rows of guns and cross bows, and at the counter was a glass display case with pistols and knives. There was some serious hunting and killing equipment available for purchase. She was amazed that such things could be bought by the general public. She must have triggered a buzzer or some kind of silent alarm when she entered because a man immediately came out from a room concealed by a curtain across the doorway.

He was a rather grizzly looking chap who wore paramilitary clothing that suggested he had just emerged from a doomsday bunker.

He looked her up and down and then said, "Can I help you?"

"Um...," she said. She had to think quickly.

"My boyfriend wants some bullets for his gun," she said.

"Sure," the man said. "Do you know what kind of bullets he's wanting?"

"They are 9MM bullets," she said.

"OK, what kind of gun is he using?" he asked.

"Oh, it's a Berretta 92FS... so he tells me," she said as she tried to hide her nervousness.

"That's a pretty serious piece of equipment your boyfriends got. What is he a cop or a security guard or something?" he asked.

"Yeah, something like that," she said.

He went to the shelf behind him and got two boxes and put them on the counter."

"I've got boxes of twenty and of fifty rounds. Do you want solids or hollows?" he asked.

She assumed that rounds meant bullets, but other than that she had no idea what he was talking about.

She said, "Which ones do you suggest, the solids or the hollows?" she asked.

"Well, that all depends on what he is shooting, and what kind of a mess he wants to make of it. If it is just target practice, then I'd go with the solids, but if he wants to blast the shit out of something, or someone, then the hollows," he said with a glint of excitement.

"I think he would want the solids, maybe a box of fifty," she said, and then finished with a smile.

"That's going to be $99.95, and I'm going to need to see a gun license, or some other identification," he said very casually, as if he asked the same of everyone.

She started to feel flushed and stupid. Of course, she had to have some kind of identification or a license. How was this going to work, she wanted to remain anonymous. She just wanted the bullets and then to get out of the shop as quickly as she could.

"I don't have my I.D. on me," she said. "How about I give you $150 cash?" and she pulled out the money and confidently slapped it down onto the counter.

"Well, I suppose if you put it like that, then maybe you could have the bullets, but I didn't see you in here," he said, once again as if he had said it many times before. He put them in a brown paper bag and handed them to her saying,

"You have a good day," as he watched her walk out of the store.

She walked briskly back to the car, keeping her head down and the paper bag clutched close. Again, she felt naughty, and even guilty as if she had committed a crime. Well, she probably just had. When she got home, she put the bullets in the drawer next to the gun and then locked it, as if locking away her dirty secret. For some reason, now that she had the bullets, the gun released its grip on her mind, and she could focus on other things. It was as if the monster had been appeased.

Ophelia spent that night at home by herself. Trey messaged her twice to check how she was doing, and before sunset she had seen a police car drive past. Later in the evening she was pretty sure that it drove past again. The cows had been moved out of her paddock and the gate to the dairy was closed. This was because her front gate had been left open, and Reggie didn't know what was going on, so he pulled the cows out. She messaged him that afternoon explaining that there was an emergency and that she had to go away for a couple of days. Of course, she did not elaborate on the nature of the emergency, and he didn't ask.

With no cows in her paddock, it was quiet, and she had to admit to herself that she actually missed their noises and eccentric behavior.

The following day, around midday, the gun

started calling to her again. She opened the drawer, took it out and looked at it, turning it over in her hand. A lifeless inanimate object. Just a hunk of machined steel, and yet, it could wield so much power and destruction. It turned her from a relatively frail and timid person, to an equal with the most dangerous and ruthless people on the planet. She could now see why psychopaths and crime bosses get guns, and how they become so dangerous. No longer were they limited by their human frailty, but instead they are able to live out their fantasies and put force to their delusions. The weapon multiplied their evil.

She desperately wanted to pull the trigger. It just hung there within its guard, created for one sole purpose; to be pulled. She wanted to feel how much recoil it had and to hear how loud it was. She wanted to see what happened to something when it was struck by a bullet. And most of all, she wanted to see if she *could* use it, and *could* actually hit something. What would be the point in having it to defend herself if she couldn't even fire the damn thing. She decided that she needed to go somewhere secluded and try it out. Somewhere far away where no one would hear or see her practicing.

She jumped in the pickup and headed deep into the mountains. It was rugged country and there were no farms or animals within sight or sound. The gun and ammo were in a sports bag on the passenger seat. She found a secluded spot, stopped, and climbed out of the vehicle with the bag, She then walked through bushland until she reached the base of a cliff. Her logic was that she could shoot toward the rock wall, and that way the bullets wouldn't be heading to anywhere that could be a risk.

She didn't really want to be doing this without Trey, but on the other hand she didn't want to get him involved either. He would either talk her out of it, or he would be implicated in whatever crime she was committing or may commit. She was a lawyer, she should know what code was being violated, and the subsequent penalty, but she did not, and she avoided looking it up or thinking about it.

She took the gun out of the bag and looked at it. There was a safety, she knew that much from watching movies, so she clicked it and now the safety was off. There was a tree growing at the base of the cliff. It had some marks on the trunk that she could use as targets. She stood about 20 meters away, figuring if she was going to shoot anyone, then that would be as close as she would want them to get to her. She raised the gun and aimed, holding it firmly with both hands. It seemed simple enough, so she tightened her grip and squeezed the trigger.

It was loud. Very loud. And it seemed to echo in the hills around her. If anyone was nearby, they would certainly hear her, even if they couldn't see her. The gun bucked up, but not too far. She had better control over it than she expected. However, she must have closed her eyes because she didn't see where the bullet struck. There did not seem to be any new marks on the tree trunk, so it must not have hit the tree.

She aimed the gun again, this time being conscious about keeping her eyes open. Again, she fired the gun, and this time she saw a splinter of wood fly off the tree.

Excellent she thought.

The tree was about as wide as a human, so if she was aiming for one, then she would have hit them, even if it was just a graze.

She then tried the used the gun as a semi-automatic, firing one bullet immediately after another. Within the first minute she emptied the magazine. She worked out how to remove the clip and replace it with a full one.

She then started to shoot at different targets, some closer, some further away. It was empowering and fun. She went through that clip in short time as she gained confidence. The last few shots were even fired from her hip without aiming and she still hit the tree trunk. She wasn't perfect, but she was competent. That would be enough for today, and figured she could come back in a few days and practice some more. She realized that what she was doing was highly illegal, and socially irresponsible, but she reasoned that the people who would condemn her had probably never been hunted by armed assassins.

So, having let off over forty rounds in quick succession, she got back into the pickup and hightailed out before anyone came to investigate. Maybe next time she would draw a target on some cardboard and bring it with her, just so she could gauge her progress. The makeshift shooting range was about 45 minutes from the cottage, so by the time she returned it was getting late in the afternoon. She was expecting Trey that evening for dinner, so she re-loaded the empty clips and then took everything upstairs and hid it in her bedroom wardrobe.

CHAPTER 18

Ophelia had picked up two huge tomahawk beef steaks when in town and had cooked them to perfection along with roasted vegetables and gravy. Trey brought more wine to add to her collection, and they opened an earthy Coonawarra Cabernet Sauvignon. It was one of those meals where, by the time you had finished, you needed to undo the top button on your jeans.

Then she brought out desert. Oh my god. She had made an old fashion treacle pudding drizzled with homemade custard. She was trying her best to out-do Trey and his open-fire cooking. They were only able to fit it into their stomachs because it tasted so good, but it was an effort. Afterward, all they could do was retire to the lounge and repose in the large chairs. To eat like this for a week would have seen them both stack on the kilograms, so she vowed to only eat salad for the next few days.

Out of the blue Ophelia asked, "Trey, do you own a gun?"

"Yes, I have a couple," he said. "I used to go shooting with my mates when I was younger. Now, I just keep them because from time to time we get foxes, wild dogs, and sometimes wild pigs on the property. So, for the safety of hikers, and for the sake of land management, we try to keep the numbers down."

"What does Francesca think of that? She strikes me as a vegan, animal rights kind of person," she said.

"I don't think she cares. She knows it goes on but has never said anything. I kind of get the feeling she's only into animal rights if they are cute and cuddly, or if she is in front of the right audience," he said with a smirk.

"Yes, that's the impression I get, and I don't even know her very well," Ophelia replied.

Then she asked, "What about a pistol? Have you ever owned or fired one?"

"No, I can't say I have," he said. "To me it seems like too much trouble getting and maintaining a license for one. I'd have to join a pistol club and do regular shooting. It's much easier to have a rifle and a shotgun, they do the job that I need to do."

"How would a rifle do against those hitmen that chased Stella and me? Do you think that maybe I should get a gun, like a rifle, or maybe even a pistol?" she asked.

"I suppose it comes down to personal choice, what you are prepared to do to get and keep a license, and what you are prepared to do with a gun in an emergency situation. I mean, would you have stayed and had a shoot-out here at the cottage if you did have a gun? Those guys were professionals, maybe even ex-military, or security. They have probably been training for years, with good quality high-powered weapons. I think you did the smartest thing by getting out of here."

"But we were extremely lucky to get out. It could have gone either way, and if we couldn't get out, then I would have liked to have a way to defend myself, besides an old axe handle," she said.

"Well, then you have the issue of close quarters defense versus long distance. If you want to stop them at a distance, then a rifle is the go, especially if you have telescopic sights and the jump on them. They are far more accurate than a pistol. However, if the intruders are already in the house, then maybe a shot gun or a pistol is the go. Probably, for someone like you a 12-gauge, or a smaller 410 shotgun is the go. You don't have to worry about aiming, it's just point and shoot. I don't think you would be comfortable handling a pistol. Maybe you could handle a small .22 caliber, but definitely not something like a 9MM," he said.

If he only knew what she had been up to earlier in the day, but she bit her lip.

She changed the conversation to getting the pickup truck fixed.

"It's a shame the authorities want to keep the whole incident hushed up. Your pickup looks pretty cool with a line of bullet holes down the side of it. You could be the famous outlaw lady from

Lavender Cottage," he said with a laugh.

"No, I'd rather get it patched up and forget the whole incident," she said.

"There is a body shop in town. I know the guy and could probably get it fixed up without anyone knowing. And if anyone does ask any questions, then maybe we could say that it was a hunting accident or something, like we did with the hikers at the cabin," he suggested.

"Yes, that sounds like a good plan. Could you set it up for me?" she asked.

"Sure, I can handle the whole thing if you like. He can probably do it out of hours. I'm pretty sure it could get fixed pretty quickly. The only thing they would have to wait on is delivery of a new rear window. Other than that, everything else is just patch and paint."

It was nice to have someone to share the burden with. Although, she was starting to feel a bit guilty. He just kept giving while she kept taking. Well, at least she fed him well, and he did get the friends with benefits thing.

On that topic, "Will you be staying tonight?" she asked in a coy voice.

"Do you want me to stay? he replied.

'Damn it' she thought. Don't reply like you're asking permission. Just tell me you are staying. Then she thought that maybe she was being a bit unfair. He probably didn't want to rush her, just like she didn't want to rush him. It was that delicate ballet at the start of all relationships.

"Do you want to stay?" she asked.

"Yes, of course, I want to stay. I always want to stay, that goes without saying. I just don't want to overstay my welcome," he said.

"You are welcome, and you can stay," she said with a smile.

They locked everything up and went to her bedroom where they sat in bed and talked by the light of the fire. She really needed to get the cottage better insulated. She was burning though a lot of firewood to keep it at the temperature she was most comfortable with. Maybe Trey could handle it at a lower temperature, but for her, she wanted it toasty warm, so she didn't have to walk around inside wearing gloves and a woolen jumper.

They had been asleep for a couple of hours. The fire was still alight, but it was just glowing coals rather than flames. Ophelia woke up to find Trey standing near the bed looking toward the doorway.

She said in a low voice, "Trey, what is it?"

In a hushed voice he replied, "I thought I heard a noise downstairs."

"There are always noises around here. It's probably the cows outside or creaking from the roof timbers and woodstove."

"I thought the cows were back in the dairy paddock?" he said.

Yes, that was right they weren't around the

cottage anymore.

He said, "You stay here, I'll have a quick look. Like you say, it's probably nothing, but I will check and make sure."

She sat up in bed and watched him creep out of the bedroom, and then disappear into the dark hallway. When he reached the top of the stairs, he turned on the light. He would have been looking from the top of the stairs down into the darkness below. She heard the wood creak as he slowly descended.

It was quiet for a long time. It became disconcerting, given the size of the cottage and the very few rooms that were downstairs. Maybe he was looking outside, perhaps peeping thought the curtains? He could have turned on the outside light to see if there was anything in the yard. Or maybe he had gone outside, although she thought she would have heard the sound of the door opening. And anyway, he was not wearing enough clothes to go outside. At least not for this long.

She waited and waited. Maybe it was only a minute or two, but it seemed like much longer. Then she looked at the wardrobe. The gun was calling her. Maybe she should get the gun, just in case. She could have it with her for protection. She wouldn't have to show it. Trey wouldn't need to know. She could keep it under the sheets, or pillow, and then when all this was over, she could slip it into the draw of her nightstand. It would be her little secret, no one else had to know.

Silently she slipped out of bed and soft-footed to the wardrobe. It was on the top shelf under a neatly folded blanket. She slid he hand in and it went straight around the grip. With the other hand she retrieved the extra clips and then she closed the wardrobe. There she stood, not knowing what to do next. She could get back into bed and patiently wait for Trey. No, that would be silly. What if he wasn't back within a minute or so? She would have to get straight back up again and investigate. But she didn't want him to see her standing there with the gun. Thus, she decided to get dressed, putting on Ugg boots, track pants, and a large wool lined jacket. Now she could hide the gun in the jacket pocket and a clip in each of her boots.

She slowly and carefully walked out into the hallway but stayed back from the top of the stairs while she listened. She though she heard a whisper, it was very faint and then there was silence. She continued to listen and then she heard it again. It sounded like Trey and another man. That other man had an accent, and it sounded something like Stella's accent.

She crept back into the bedroom and very carefully closed the door. There was definitely someone else down there apart from Trey. And they were definitely whispering.

So, she had to come to a decision on the spot. Was Trey being held hostage, as in he had a gun to his head, or was he working with them?

No, the later couldn't be true, that was just too ridiculous to contemplate. She had met Trey before Stella was even on the scene, and he had helped them and hidden them when they were being chased. Therefore, it must be the first option. He was being held at gunpoint by assassins.

But still this was all so ridiculous, why would they risk coming back here, especially now that Stella was gone? Was there something that Stella had said to her that she didn't realize was so important? Or maybe Stella had left something here that they were looking for, that she hadn't yet discovered? It might even be the gun, she thought as she looked at it in her hand.

Then Ophelia looked at the balcony. Should she escape through there again, or would they be expecting that? Maybe they hadn't realized last time that it was the way they had escaped. Should she risk it, given the only other option was going down the stairs, and surely that is what they would be expecting? Their plan would likely be to keep Trey silent downstairs and wait for her to come down and investigate. Then they would have both of them.

She started to run through movie plots in her head. They would both get tied up and then interrogated, maybe even tortured, until the villains got what they wanted; something like a Bond movie. But what did they want? She had no clue.

Or perhaps the objective was to kill her, or both of them outright. But that didn't make sense, because if they did, then they would have just come straight up to the bedroom and shot her while she lay in bed. And as for Trey, he probably would have been shot on sight.

Perhaps they hadn't shot Trey, or her, because they knew that she had the gun. That changed the dynamic. They wouldn't just barge into her room if they thought she was armed and prepared to shoot.

Thus, she built the narrative in her mind that it was going to be a shoot-out, and the winner would be decided on tactics, that is, who outsmarted who. That was a playing field she could win on. She was a lawyer, and now so much more, so she was smart and capable. Secondly, she was in her cottage on her property, so she had the home advantage. Thirdly, they could not be sure if she had the gun or be confident she knew how to use it.

She put the spare bullets into her pocket, grabbed a small flashlight, and then once again slipped out onto the balcony, locking the door behind her.

This time she was better prepared and wore gloves, scarf, and beanie. She also knew the distances she needed to drop between the levels, thus the descent was quick, quiet, and efficient, like a ninja. The outside lights were off, and instead of immediately trying to look through the windows, first she went wide and circled the cottage. She wanted to see if there were any other villains waiting in the shadows. She couldn't see anyone and gambled that they were inside, be that one or several.

She went back to the cottage, going window to window trying to peep in. It seemed that the curtains had been disturbed on one window and she could see the drama inside.

Trey was sitting on a seat in the kitchen, his hands and legs were being bound to a chair and his mouth was gagged. The assailant was just putting the final touches to his bindings. There was another man standing near them, he was holding a gun like hers, but it was pointed toward the stairs rather than at Trey.

She got 'her' gun out of the jacket pocket and released the safety. She would only get the chance to shoot one of them before the element of surprise was lost. Did she have the guts, or the right, to shoot them, and where should she aim? It was all very good to be an armchair analyst and say, 'Oh yeah, just shoot them in the shoulder or the leg. Make it a disabling shot that doesn't kill them. Then you can call the police and ambulance and the bad guys get taken away to face justice.'

No, it wasn't like that. If she only wounded them then they would probably continue to fight back. They were trained to keep going even when wounded, they'd grit their teeth, shoot back, and then limp or crawl to their car and escape.

God, it would have been nice if she could have just scared them away. Like maybe firing a warning shot, and with that they up and left the cottage and never returned. But it wasn't going to be like that. She had to shoot with the intention to kill. Granted, her shot may not kill them, indeed her aim may be so poor that even if she did hit them, it may only be a grazing shot, or what they call a flesh wound.

Regardless, she had to do something right now, before the man dealing with Trey finished and they moved out of target range. She elected to shoot at the one that was furthest away from Trey, the one with his gun already out. He was the one that would likely respond first once she revealed herself. And if she missed him, at least there was less chance of her hitting Trey.

She didn't know anything about shooting through glass, only that bullets went through glass. They had gone through the window when Sella was shot at, and they had also gone through the window of the pickup. But what would happen if she fired the gun when it was up close to the window? Would it affect the aim? Would fragments of glass blow back into her face blinding her? She had seen in movies where they smashed the glass first and then fired through the opening. She couldn't do that, or she would lose the element of surprise.

She was assuming the backdoor was locked, but

only because she had locked it earlier in the night. The hitmen may have unlocked it, she couldn't be sure. Thus, she thought, what if she went to the back door, slowly opened it, and then shot through the partial opening? Both of the men would have their backs to her. She could get in a second shot, maybe, and if they tried to dive out of the way she would be able to follow them. It was a bolder strategy, but it had the greater chance for success.

CHAPTER 19

Ophelia crept around to the back door. Crouching down and holding the gun in one hand, she reached for the handle with the other. Slowly, she pulled down and it moved. It must have been how they had got into the cottage. It was a relatively old and unsophisticated lock, so perhaps they had picked it. The latching mechanism was silent, which was a great relief. If it had clicked or creaked, then they would have shot her straight through the wood of door.

She carefully pushed it, and again it was silent. Indeed, when she had first moved into the cottage all of the doors and windows were stiff and creaked from neglect, so she had oiled them. Through the gap that opened between the door and the fame, she saw Trey. It was a side-on profile. Then she saw the man closest to him, and finally the other man. She took aim at the second man who was furthest away and standing upright. Her intention was to hit him square in the center of his back. She carefully aimed the gun, held it as firmly as she could, and then she squeezed the trigger.

There was a loud noise and the gun recoiled back

toward her, just grazing her face but not causing any injury. She refocused her eyes and saw that the man had fallen forward onto the floor. He was still moving. She had hit him in his shoulder blade. It was probably not going to be a fatal, but then again what did she know? Maybe he could die from loss of blood or something. But still he moved and was slowly turning holding his gun, within a short time he would be facing her.

The man who was closest to Trey had jumped and was now in the corner of the kitchen, crouched on the floor with his gun out. He had not noticed the back door was ajar and was still trying to assess where the shot had come from. Quickly, she took aim and fired at him. She was aiming for the center of his chest but instead hit him in the upper arm. It was the same one that held his gun, causing it to drop to the floor. She fired another shot at him, and this time she hit him in the hip, and he rolled over onto the floor.

By this time the first man had spied her, but instead of pointing his gun at her, he pointed it at Trey. There Trey sat, bound and gagged in the middle of a firefight, an innocent helpless witness to the carnage. Then to her disbelief the man fired a bullet into Trey. He reeled back in the seat and fell backwards to the floor. It was likely Trey banged his head hard on the stone floor, and he now appeared to be unconscious.

She wanted to run straight over to Trey, but

she was smarter than that. She ran straight over to the man who had just shot Trey, stamped her foot down on his arm and kept doing it until he released the gun. She kicked it away and went to the other man and also kicked his gun away, although like Trey, the other man did not move. Keeping her gun on the still conscious man, she went over to Trey. He had been shot in the shoulder, but it was lower than the other shoulder shot. Her knowledge of anatomy wasn't the best, but she was thinking it may be a bit too close to vital organs. She tried to untie him, but they had used tape, and it was difficult to undo. So, she ran over to a drawer and got out a large knife and cut the tape. The gag in his mouth had also been taped into place and she had to cut it without jabbing him.

As she moved his head, she noticed his hair was wet with blood. It got onto her hands and was pooling on the floor. He seemed to be bleeding badly from the back of the head where it had hit the floor. She grabbed a nearby towel and wrapped it around his head, and then grabbed the tape that had been left on the table and wrapped it around the bandage to apply extra pressure. It was just instinctual because she didn't really know what she was doing, or why. He still had the wound in his shoulder, but that didn't seem to be bleeding as much, so she would get to that shortly.

She needed to call the police and an ambulance. Damn, her phone was upstairs next to the bed. She went over to the still conscious man and began taping up his legs, and then rolled him onto his front and taped his hands behind his back. All this time she hadn't spoken, as if she was that silent assassin. But then she spoke to him.

She said, "I don't know why you came back. I don't know anything or anyone."

He said in a strong accent, "Yes you do. You saw my face and have my gun. That is too many loose ends that must be cleaned up."

"Well looks like you messed up buddy," she said, and then spoke no more.

He just laughed and said, "We'll see," in an arrogant tone.

She could understand him shooting at her, but why on Earth did he have to go and shoot Trey? He knew less than her. Was it just to be malicious, or maybe it was to slow her down? Perhaps, he thought she would lose her composure if she saw Trey get shot. It was the only thing that she could think of. But she hadn't lost her composure, and now she had both of them. She picked up their guns, ran upstairs, got her phone, and then came back down. After calling the police, she did what she could to patch up the hole in Trey's shoulder, as well as the holes she had put in the two intruders.

The police and ambulance arrive at the same time. The hitmen had cut the chain for the gate and driven silently all the way down the driveway. This was fortunate because it allowed the emergency vehicles to park right next to the cottage. Trey was alive but he seemed to have lost a lot of blood and was in a bad way. The two hitmen suffered lesser injuries, and both were conscious by the time they were taken away in separate ambulances.

Ophelia could not accompany Trey to the hospital, regardless of how much she protested. The police had too many questions for her, and they wanted answers while everything was fresh. Fortunately, she knew the police, and they knew her. They were the same officers that had dealt with the first attack, so they understood her motives.

But still, there was the issue of her having, and using, the gun. A prosecutor could argue that she possessed the gun with intent, because she had knowingly concealed it, practiced with it, and had even purchased additional bullets. Under the State's firearms laws there was the potential for her to face up to 13 years imprisonment. On top of that she could face hefty fines for non-compliance, and multiple assaults occasioning bodily harm.

For sure there was no doubt it was self-defense, but the law can be a bit more complicated than that. She, more than anyone, knew that. Australia does not have Castle Doctrine law that permits deadly force to be used under certain circumstances of trespass and home invasion. Thus, she would have to rely on an argument of reasonable force and foreseeable danger. But because she was already outside of the house, and was not being actively pursued by the intruders, her line of argument would need to be that she reacted to an immediate threat to Trey. Ironically, if the intruders had not shot Trey, then her argument would have been weaker.

The police station was located near the hospital. She followed the police to the station in her own vehicle, filled out a few forms, was photographed and fingerprinted, and then was allowed to go. It was after midnight before she got to see Trey. He had just come out of a surgery to remove the bullet. It had broken a rib, but miraculously the bullet had missed vital organs. Thankfully the hitmen had not used hollow point bullets, or it would have been a lot messier, and possibly fatal.

However, the doctors were concerned about his head. He had a hairline fracture of his skull, and consequently a cerebral edema. It was a serious condition that could cause long term effects, including memory loss through to brain damage. They were keeping him in an induced coma until the swelling subsided.

She sat in his room and the nurses and doctors came in and out through the early hours of the morning. She was too amped-up to sleep, and instead drank coffee. How could such a perfect night have gone so sour? All she could say to herself was that it could have been so much worse.

Despite the caffeine, and the hospital

surroundings, before dawn she fell asleep in the chair next to Trey's bed. A nurse put a blanket over her, and then left her to also recover from the ordeal. When she woke it was mid-morning and nurses were fussing over Treys tubes and recording his vitals. He still lay unresponsive. Apart from the bandage on his head, he looked just like he was peacefully sleeping, as he had done on previous nights when she had secretly watched him.

The doctors couldn't give her much information regarding his condition. All they could say was that he was stable and that it would take time. They said that he would probably be unresponsive for at least another 24 hours, and then depending on his condition, they would try to wake him up. It was suggested that she go home, and they would alert her of any change. The staff were kind and sympathetic, and she trusted that they would do this. So, reluctantly, she left his bedside and drove home.

The crime scene investigators had already been and gone. They had left a note for her which included permission to clean up the blood on the floor and various splatters about the kitchen.

She had been tough and stoic through everything. The move to the country, the financial insecurity, the escape with Stella and then the hiding out, and now this shootout. She had held it all together and been strong for herself and for everyone around her. But now, with Trey comatose in hospital, and sitting all alone on the kitchen floor with a scrubbing brush and bucket of bleach, she began to feel sorry for herself. She curled up into the smallest ball she could make and cried.

That afternoon an electrician came and put extra lighting around the outside of the house, including the vehicle shed and down by the woodshed. Not that it would make much difference when dealing with professional hitmen, but at least it was a first line of defense. A locksmith also came, and they upgraded all the locks on the doors and windows. Once again, a determined intruder could still get in, but it would be more difficult and noisier for them to do so now.

Still, this was not the direction she had planned. In the country many people didn't even lock their back doors. It was supposed to be a safe and peaceful place to live, and for the most part it was. Even as meth-fueled crime affected other rural communities, there was little to no evidence of it in this region. Instead, it still had a semblance of that old country way of life and values, as objectionably conservative as they may sometimes be.

While sitting in the kitchen she heard the sound of a motorbike pulling up to her back door. She opened it to find Reggie climbing off his motorbike and then removing something from the plastic milk crate he permanently strapped to the back of the bike.

He said, "Hi there, heard you've had a bit

of trouble so we thought you may appreciate something." News traveled fast in a small country town.

She invited him in, and after he took of his muddy boots, he carried in a basket and put it on the table. Inside was a freshly baked cake. He said that it was his wife's award-winning sponge cake, along with some of her homemade pickles and chutneys. He also included a couple of liters of fresh milk. She couldn't help but break into tears again. He gave her a big hug and then set to making a cup of tea from the kettle that sat at a permanent boil on the woodstove.

The police had given her permission to talk about the events, although there were some details she was still not allowed to discuss. So, Reggie sat at the kitchen table while she unloaded her story, just listening and nodding. He assured her that nothing like this had ever happened in their community before and was not likely to happen again. It was just a freaky thing and that she shouldn't let it shape her view of how safe and peaceful it was living here. Also, that she shouldn't underestimate the support she would get from the community, and to accept help when it was offered. He reinforced that she didn't have to go through this alone.

Ophelia didn't want to sleep alone in the cottage, not while everything was so raw. So, she packed an overnight bag and went back to the hospital.

Trey's condition was unchanged, as he lay there unresponsive. She brought in some of the things Reggie had delivered, and other items of her own, in the hope that Trey would wake up in the morning and she could feed him. She pulled the chair up next to his bed, made herself comfortable, and then fell asleep.

CHAPTER 20

When Ophelia woke the following morning, Francesca was sitting opposite her and immediately got up and made her a coffee.

"Good morning, how are you?" Francesca asked in a friendly voice.

Ophelia was still groggy and disorientated, but said,

"I am well, thank you. How is Trey, has he woken up yet?"

"No, he is still unconscious, but the doctors say his condition has improved. The swelling has reduced, and they will try to wake him up later today."

"That is good news. I have been so worried," Ophelia said.

"The nurses tell me that you have been here for the past two nights. That was very thoughtful of you," Francesca said.

Ophelia didn't quite know how to respond. There were a couple of reasons why she watched over Trey. Firstly, because she felt responsible for his condition. If it wasn't for her, all of this wouldn't have happened, and he would be going about his normal life. And secondly, he was now her boyfriend, well at least that is what she believed. She desperately wanted to be here, even if that may be interpreted as being for her own selfish reasons, because she wanted to be here when he woke up. She held the romantic notion that she would be the first person he saw, and that he would be forever grateful for her commitment and vigilance. Was that selfish or was it just how relationships worked?

Francesca then said, "Trey spoke to me about his relationship with you and scolded me for how I have treated you. He was right to do so, and I am sorry for how I behaved."

Ophelia listened but didn't say anything. She was reserving judgement, not knowing if she was genuine or just trying to make the best of an embarrassing situation.

Francesca continued, "I didn't trust you. There have been so many times in the past when girls threw themselves at Trey, and even stalked him, and I just assumed you were like them. But now I see that you are different and that you have feelings for each other. I will admit that I am a little jealous. I have to face up to the reality that nothing has, or will, happen between Trey and me, even though we have known each other for many years. It just wasn't meant to be."

Francesca said, "He talked about how you were different, that you were real, as opposed to fake, and how you were very strong and determined. He liked the dreams that you had, and your plans for developing your business. He felt like he had found a kindred spirit, maybe even a soul mate."

Ophelia felt a little bashful as she sipped her coffee and listened.

"You are very lucky, and I hope you can see that," Francesca said. "I really hope that you treat him as well as I know he will treat you. Please don't break his heart, he doesn't deserve that. Underneath that tough and confident exterior is a sweet little boy who is looking for love, just like I hope you are."

Then Francesca said, "The police came to the lodge and asked some questions and did some looking around. They told me about what had happened, including how you had a shootout with some organized-crime guys. That must have taken a lot of guts. I don't know how you managed it, but I'm sure your actions saved Trey's life.

"So please don't blame yourself for his condition. He was with you because that is where he wanted to be, not because you asked. And from what I know of him, he would have taken a bullet for you if that was the way things went down."

Ophelia said, "Thank you, yes, I have been blaming myself for getting him involved. But I also realize that sometimes events spring upon you that you just couldn't see coming, and he just got caught up in everything. Perhaps, if he wasn't there, then I would have been killed, so in some way I feel in his debt because he probably saved my life."

"He put himself out there to save you, I'm sure of that," Francesca said.

"How are you managing at the lodge without him?" Ophelia asked.

"It is OK. I was able to work the roster to cover his absence. And speaking of the lodge, I need to get back. We have another corporate group arriving this afternoon and I need to make sure it runs smoothly."

She got up to leave and then said, "By the way, when you get a chance, we would take all of the produce you can make. It has become very popular. I hope you plan on expanding your business. The food and lavender products are really good."

"Thank you, yes when everything settles down, I plan to get back into full swing," Ophelia said.

Francesca smiled and said, "Call me when you are ready. Take care," and then left.

It was mid-afternoon, and the doctors were standing around Trey's bed. The propofol had been turned off and they were monitoring for any reaction. He could wake up within minutes, hours, days, or never. However, they were optimistic given the rate of his recovery. He was young and fit and had received treatment within a short time of sustaining his injuries. In fact, it was probably Ophelia's triage that saved his life.

Yet, despite their efforts to wake him, he

remained unresponsive. Progressively over the hours, each of the doctors and then nurses drifted back to their rounds and workstations. Ophelia was now alone with him as he lay under 'natural, conditions', therefore no sedative or neuromuscular blocking agents. As far as she was concerned, he was now just in a deep sleep, and he would wake up when he was ready. However, she made a point of no longer being quiet. At times she even called his name and talked to him as if he were awake, in the hope of waking him.

It was early evening and the catering service brought her a meal. It was very thoughtful that someone must have ordered it on her behalf, knowing that she was keeping vigil with nothing left to eat. It was typical hospital food, small portions and rather bland, but still she enjoyed it. When she had finished, she put the cover back over the plate and slid it onto the side table.

"Did you enjoy that?" a voice said. She jerked with surprise and looked around the room.

Then the voice said, "Here, I'm over here."

Was it a ghost? No, Trey had woken up and was watching her. She had gotten so used to him lying there unconscious that she wasn't expecting him to be speaking to her.

With a big smile she said, "Hi... How are you feeling?" and she grabbed his hand.

"I don't know yet, I'm pretty numb at the moment, but I think I'm OK," he said.

"How long have you been watching me?" she asked with embarrassment.

"Oh, probably since your second piece of broccoli. So, what? Are you doing eating my dinner?" he said with a laugh, and then a wince as he realized his chest and head hurt and were bandaged.

Ophelia called in the nurse, who in turn called the doctors. They told her that his condition looked very positive, and they were optimistic that he would make a full recovery. If he continued to improve, he could go home within the week, provided there was someone to care for him.

He did improve during the week. Ophelia came in everyday, although she no longer stayed during the nights. She explained everything that had happened on that fateful night, and how he had ended up in the hospital. His memory of the events was hazy. He did remember being tied up on the chair, but not being shot or falling backwards. He was amazed by the story about Stella getting the gun and hiding it in the pickup truck. And then Ophelia going out and practicing with it before getting into a shootout with the hitmen. He said it was a side of her that he had never imagined and jokingly vowed to never get on Ophelia's bad side.

The doctor said that it was normal that the part of Trey's memory relating to the shooting had been blanked out. With time his mind would probably recall it, but presently it was locked deep in his subconscious while the brain and mind healed themselves. It was amazing how they were both the same and different at the same time. With the mind being so much more than the sum of its parts and following a different path to repair.

She came to realize how popular Trey was within the local community, and beyond. His room had received a steady stream of visitors, and cards and flowers were everywhere.

She also met his parents, and his brother, all of whom drove up from Sydney to see him, and to also meet her. She liked his family, they were nice people, and she could see where he got his pleasant nature from. He introduced her as his girlfriend, which she really liked, and everyone charged her with looking after him, which in every case she promised to do. It seemed that she was now obligation bound to him, which happily complemented her desire to be with him.

Within the week, he was discharged, and Ophelia insisted that he stay with her. She brought him home in the truck, which had just come back from being repaired. Trey's mate had done her a solid favor and fixed it in less time than it would normally take to get just a quote. He only charged her for the materials and not for his labor, which she very much appreciated. It seemed now that she was Trey's girlfriend, and somewhat of a local hero, everyone wanted to pay their respects and help her out. Even the electrician came back and did some extra jobs around the cottage, without her asking, and without charging. Once you break into the inner circle of a country town, your family gets bigger, and life gets better.

Reggie was still supplying milk and eggs, although he warned that soon the glut would end and flip to a shortage, meaning she would have to pay for the milk. She always expected this would be the case, and so was just grateful for the extra profit while she was establishing her business. However, he said the eggs would always be complementary. They were from his own chickens, and they laid far more than his wife and he knew what to do with.

They arrived back at the cottage. The cows were once again in the paddock, and the property was looking well maintained. She assisted Trey as he gingerly climbed down from the pickup, and then with his arm over her shoulder they walked the cobblestones to the front door. It was the second half of winter and the weather had changed. The breathless frosty nights had gone, now replaced by constant westerly winds. It didn't get as cold at night, but the wind went right through you and chilled to the bone.

Inside, the cottage was warm, and the kitchen looked more like it was used for a commercial operation rather than domestic. Ophelia had become very organized with a place for everything and everything in its place. She would get up well before sunrise and do her baking so that deliveries and pickups could be finished before 7am. Then she would have breakfast and afterward commence her work experimenting and producing lavender products such as essential oils, soaps and candles. She was also planning to renovate one of the outbuildings, a tumbled down barn, to be used for storage, and maybe later as a shop for tourists.

Trey helped her where he could. It was extremely handy to have someone there to make sure things didn't boil-over or burn. And someone to answer the phone, or the door, when her hands were full and covered in dough or butter. Yes, Lavender Cottage was finally heading in the direction she had dreamed. There was still lots of potential, and lots to do, and that was fine. One step at a time. She hadn't even had an official opening or done any advertising. When she did do that, she would probably have to consider employing people to help out, especially on weekends when the tourist trade would be at its busiest.

It took about four weeks for Trey to be able to drive and do light duties at the lodge. In his absence, the dynamics had changed there. He had essentially been replaced by a very competent person. It's not that Trey wasn't competent also, it's just that this other person had a range of skills that better aligned with Francesca's needs and vision for the future.

But instead of being concerned or put-out, Trey

was actually pleased. He transitioned from doing the manual work, to being more of a guide, instructor, and facilitator. He was able to draw more on the skills he had developed as a musician, especially his talent for working the crowd. He had even picked up his guitar and performed some campfire songs for guests. This greatly enhanced the 'lodge experience' for the guests, and would no doubt increase business and grow the bottom line.

Ophelia and Trey never discussed whether he would move back to the lodge. Indeed, the lodge was becoming so busy that they regularly rented out his old cabin, and his possessions were either moved into a storage shed, or increasingly arriving at the Ophelia's cottage. She just assumed he would be staying with her for now, and maybe forever. It was pragmatic and romantic at the same time. But it was not that he was freeloading. He was actually far wealthier than her, but this was never factored into her decisions, or her business plans. She was determined to make it, using her own skills and merit, and within her own budget. He respected that and never dangled carrots in front of her, never encouraging her to spend money that she would otherwise have not spent. But this didn't mean he did not buy nice things for her, or them, from time to time. He did like to spoil her when he could, and she liked it.

CHAPTER 21

A few months had passed, and it was now mid-spring. The days were warming fast, and the parade of afternoon thunderstorms had begun. Ophelia was preparing for the official opening to the public. A campaign had been organized that included a website, social media, as well as local flyers and print advertising.

She had a sign ready to be placed at the front gate that advertised Lavender Cottage, along with the opening hours. Reggie had come over with a tractor and levelled the driveway, and built up a visitor's carpark, all paved with fresh white gravel. Renovation work had also been completed on the barn which was now a shop and café specializing in scones, cheeses, and cakes.

The lavender was coming into full bloom and presented a magical scene, with rows of purple flowers stretching from the old stone wall at the front of the property, down to the cottage. It was a provincial picture waiting to be painted. The flowers fed the bees, and not just the couple of hives that she had got from Trey, but the many more she had acquired since. Trey had taught her how to manage the bees, and it became a significant part of her business. They were starting to pot their lavender honey and it was in high demand across the country. When Trey wasn't working at the lodge, he was unofficially in charge of managing the bees and honey. It was good for his recuperation, and it freed Ophelia up for her so many other projects.

For the grand opening, Trey suggested they have a Saturday afternoon through to evening party, and invite folk from the surrounding towns. It would be a tailgate party out in the paddock. There would pits, grills, and smokers, cooking Texas-style BBQ. In cattle country, there was no problem getting meat at bargain prices, and in some cases, donated. They certainly had the room to do it, and now with the weather warming up, provided there wasn't a thunderstorm, the evenings would be warm, clear, and perfect.

Ophelia and Trey walked next door to the winery to see if they also wanted to participate. They climbed through the fence and wove their way down through the vines. They were now bursting forth with growth, and fragrant with blossom. Although she had lived next door for a few months, it was her first time formally visiting the complex. It comprised old buildings like on her property, but also very modern facilities including a glass fronted reception and tasting building.

They met with two of the winery managers and enjoyed a sampling of their produce. It was brought to their attention that the winery sold some of her cheese, as well as lavender candles in their gift shop. The candles were made from her on-farm bees wax, infused with lavender oil. The winery was very keen to be a part of the event and were prepared to set up a stall that promoted their products, and also sold to the public.

They said that they could take care of all the licensing requirements, and they also had some suggestions regarding other local producers that may want to be present on the day and set up a stall. The way it was shaping up, it was going to be more like a country fair than just a BBQ and launching for Lavender Cottage.

It was also suggested that maybe music could be organized, such as a live band. This got Trey thinking and he said, "Leave that to me. I'm sure I can rope in some old friends and put together a show."

Thus, the event was growing in size and scope, which was a good thing, because it would put Lavender Cottage on the map. Maybe they could even make it an annual event? With the winery on one side, the dairy on two, and a commercial orchard across the road, it wasn't like they would be disturbing anyone. So, provided they had adequate lighting and facilities, then they were not likely to have any problems getting local council approval.

The date was set for one week's time, and everything was falling into place.

Ophelia now had two girls working with her, Jenna and Alison. Both of them were locals that had just left school. Jenna worked in the bakery and café side of the business and Alison with the lavender and honey products. They were young, fresh, and enthusiastic. Ophelia paid and treated them well. She would call them her girls with a sense of pride. If one were to add up all of the work that Trey did around the business, then effectively it had gone from one person's dream and efforts to a business that employed four people full-time, just within a few months. And at the current rate of growth, she would need to put on more people to keep up with demand.

Ophelia was no capitalist, and neither did she have a background in economics or accounting, but she was very savvy when it came to producing what people wanted and doing that to the highest quality. She did not offer a wide range of products, but what she did do was of exceptional quality. Thus, whatever she touched usually turned to gold. Of course, it helped that Trey had experience in dealing with tour groups and public relations. They were a super couple.

Something unique to Lavender Cottage was that everything was prepared using old woodstoves. There was, of course, the trusty woodstove in the cottage, but then she acquired two more from salvage sales that were incorporated into the renovated barn. They contributed to the unique flavor of her products, and to the olde world ambiance of Lavender Cottage. As they ran day and night, from autumn to spring they would keep everything warm, and over the summer months the buildings could be opened up to the breeze.

Although they hadn't had the official opening, there was already a steady stream of tourists. When people stopped at the winery, they would also visit Lavender Cottage, and to help with this, they had built a path from the winery boundary that took tourists under the grand oak tree, through the lavender, and then along the cobblestone path to the renovated barn shop.

The day of the official opening arrived. Many of the locals had turned up and their pickup trucks were parked in rows with people sitting in the trays. There were many firepits and BBQs, as well as stalls from various local businesses. It was like a medieval fair but with electrical lighting, modern music, and pickup trucks. The air was filled with the fragrance of lavender and cooked meat.

Trey had gotten his old band back together, as well as some other local musicians. The warm-up acts had played and shortly Trey would be going on stage. For the past hour or so he had been busy doing the set-up and conferring with his fellow musicians. He said to Ophelia he had a surprise for her, but he wouldn't say any more than that. She had no idea what to expect but was apprehensive he may do or say something in front of the crowd that could embarrass her. No, surely, he wouldn't do that she thought, trying to reassure herself.

She sat on the back of her truck managing a ridiculously big, and thoroughly enjoyable, hamburger, and surveying the happy scene. She marveled at how far they had come in such a short time, and how wonderful this event would be for promoting her business. Then, amongst the people chatting around her she heard a familiar seductive Mediterranean voice.

"Hello Ophelia."

She turned to find Stella approaching.

"Oh my God," Ophelia cried out, putting down her burger and jumping up to give Stella a hug. Then she stood back and looked at her.

It was that same Latin beauty. She was dressed as if she had just come from a Spanish 'doma vaquera', a prestigious dressage, and her Andalusian stallion was being stabled and brushed somewhere by a country boy. She wore a flat brimmed black hat, black straight-cut blazer with gold buttons, a Ferrari-red pleated skirt, and black high-heeled gaucho boots. Her hair was in a long single braid and tied with a matching red ribbon. She could have just come from a photo shoot promoting Madeira, Dior, or Maserati. It seemed this woman could take on any identity or situation and own it. She must have heard that tonight was an outdoors 'country' event, thus dressed appropriately. The Femme Fatale of her own Spaghetti Western.

She was accompanied by an extremely handsome unshaven man wearing what looked like an Amani suit. Yet, he remained aloof, as if he was a bodyguard. Stella introduced him as Migel but did not hang off him as other women would likely do, given the adonis that he was. He stood proud, yet obedient, as her other imaginary stallion.

Ophelia said, "How did you know about the opening?"

"It was on your internet site. I have followed your progress. I am very pleased that you have done so well. I was also told about your troubles, and how the sicario returned. My information tells me that you fought back. You found the pistola, yes?"

"Yes, I did, thank you. I think it saved our lives," Ophelia said.

"This is all behind you now, and you have your business. It will be good," Stella said with a smile, then continued, "And what of Trey. He is yours now?" she asked.

Ophelia understood what Stella was saying and responded, "Yes, we are together, and very happy thank you."

"And he is here with you tonight?" she asked.

"Yes, he is up on the stage. His old band is about

to play for the crowd," Ophelia said proudly.

"He is artist, this I did not know. You have a man with passion. This is a good balance for you, but hold on tight, the other women will also want him."

Again, Ophelia knew what Stella meant and that it was not intended to provoke or destabilizer her. It was well-intentioned advice, but just delivered in Stella's direct way of talking, and her view of relationships and the world.

"So, what of yourself? Obviously, you are still in Australia. Have all of your problems finished and you are free to live your life as you wish?" Ophelia enquired.

"Yes, I have done my part, and I am now safe and free. I will leave Australia soon and return to Italy to see my family. I can be with my children and make plans for a new life," Stella said.

Just then Trey came over the speakers and welcomed everyone to the official opening of Lavender Cottage. He was very good at being the master of ceremonies and also getting the crowd fired up. His band then started their set and played old hits that the crowd sang and danced along with. For the last song of the set, he announced that he had written a new song and that he and the band had only had a few sessions to practice it. Thus, he hoped that the crowd would be sympathetic to how raw it might be. He played the acoustic guitar and the rest of the members accompanied and provided backing vocals. It was a sweet and happy tune, and based on the crowd reaction, was destined to become a hit. The song was called Ophelia.

THE END

ABOUT THE AUTHOR

Mike graduated in Environmental and Political Science, then worked for government and industry writing on climate change, food, and energy security. His background is reflected in the 'hard' science of 'Deep Sahara' and the 'Dark Earth' Sci-Fi novel series. Even in the darkest of times Mike's stories offer humanity a glimmer of hope by exploring alternative societies and futures. The Ophelia stories, however, depart from his typical genre, and span more homely and romantic themes.